I0586353

Chloe Spencer

Vicarious

A Novella

SLASHIC HORROR
PRESS

**Other titles by Chloe Spencer**

*Monstersona*
*Duality*

The characters and events in this book are fictitious. Any similarity to real persons, living or dead, is coincidental and not intended by the author.

Originally published in Australia by Slashic Horror Press in 2023.

ISBN-13: 978-0-6457638-4-3
Cover design by Ruth Anna Evans
Interior design by David-Jack Fletcher
Edited by David-Jack Fletcher

*This page left intentionally blank*

*For Cody and Aurora, who have been my lighthouses as I sailed stormy seas.*

## Content Warnings

*Vicarious* contains graphic depictions of violence, gore, blood (including menstrual blood), death (including animal death), mentions of domestic violence, depictions of stalking and attempted sexual assault, discussions of child sexual abuse, car crashes, fatphobia, homophobia and use of homophobic slurs, vomit, and consensual BDSM and edge-play.

# Prologue

Since she was small, going to the bathroom alone made Gertie Taylor fraught with anxiety. Her father had blamed her mother for this—the woman never let Gertie have a moment of peace and had accompanied her to the restroom. It became normal for Gertie to have someone with her during every mundane bowel movement, but after her mother's passing, the security she had experienced crumbled violently and all at once. Her neglectful father refused to accompany her to the restroom, insisting she was old enough to go by herself. Gertie did try—she *had* to—and when she was at home, she grew more comfortable with it.

But to Gertie, public restrooms were full of strangers lurking around corners, hiding on top of toilets, watching her through the slits in the stall doors. Her mother, a true crime fanatic, told her that predators loved to hide in bathrooms, and had insisted that this was why women should *never* go to the restroom alone. "All it takes is for one lone wolf to follow you in, lamb chop," her mother had said, as she reapplied her lipstick in the mirror. "But after that, you'll have to hope someone will hear you scream." No matter how occupied the bathroom was, Gertie always looked for figures hidden away in the shallowest of shadows. The eyes of others were red hot candles and Gertie was the wax that burned beneath their gaze. Someone—and she didn't know who—was waiting for the perfect moment to catch her off-guard and commit some sort of heinous crime. (What kind of crime, she never knew. Her mother never explained that part, just that it had something to do with her "privates".) Forced visits to the restroom alone left her with panic attacks that left her unable to cope. After her mother's passing, school administrators took pity on her and assigned an aide—often another student—to accompany her. After her behaviors didn't improve, however, she was sent to the school guidance counselor once a week. This did not bode well for her image among peers, and so began the name calling.

Despite these administrative interventions, her anxiety didn't dissolve, and on occasion, it led to her having accidents in class. Too many times, she would stand with quivering lips, piss dripping down her legs, asking someone to take her to the nurse's office for a change of clothes. Her social incompetence, along with her dorky appearance (oversized glasses, knobby knees, and a baby-plump body) made her a delicious target for bullies, and Beatrice Robinson was by far the worst of them. Strawberry blond, petite, and pretty-faced, Bea was quickly welcomed by the throngs of popular girls, only to later usurp them and become the head bitch herself.

From the time she transferred to their school in the third grade, Bea made a habit of following Gertie into the bathroom. The taunting started out harmless enough—Gertie would muster the courage to go inside, and when she exited, she'd find a sink was running, as if a ghost had turned it on. It escalated to doors slamming when she was inside a stall, to rain showers of suspiciously dirty clumps of toilet paper, to flashes of cellphone cameras flickering outside the stall. Contrary to what her mother had warned her, strange men wouldn't be the ones to terrorize Gertie in the restroom.

It was a preteen girl.

When Gertie knew she was *absolutely* being watched, her fears morphed into a beast that consumed her entire daily routine. The anxiety and depression that consumed her during this era left her wishing for death, but little lamb that she was, Gertie could never inflict harm on herself that could do any damage. Her suicide ideation was strong, but just as you need a will to live, you need a will to die. This left her with no choice but to adapt. The older she got, the more strategic she was with reducing the need to use the restroom. She drank a limited amount of liquids, ate small meals that were low in fiber, and on occasion, wore extra-strength pads for added protection. She studied Bea's behaviors, learning what times her class was out at recess, gym, or in the cafeteria. Any method she could use to reduce Bea's opportunities to terrorize her was worth it in the long run, and for a number of years, this worked.

Until she got her period in the seventh grade. The damn thing was too unpredictable for her to keep up with, and to make matters worse, her horrendous cramps inspired spontaneous, disgusting shits that even the thickest and diaper-like of pads could not hope to contain. (Not that she had tried. Or would publicly admit to trying.) So once a month, Bea got her opportunity to wreak havoc. No matter how sneaky she could be, Bea would always come traipsing after her, her little singsong voice calling out her name.

"Ger-*trude*," Bea trilled, stepping into the restroom. "You know better than to run from me by now."

Gertie sighed on the other side of the stall. She quickly finished changing out her pad and attempted to open the door, but Bea pushed her back, almost tripping her over the toilet. She reached into her jeans pocket and withdrew a pair of plastic gloves, snapping them on with a wicked smile.

"S-stop it," Gertie stammered, attempting to stand. "I have to wash my hands."

Bea threw the door shut behind her, locking the two of them within the stall. There was a malicious glint in her silver eyes, one that sent Gertie's knees into a violent tremble.

She spread her arms wide and pressed her hands on either side of the stall to stop her prey from escaping.

"If you don't let me out, I'll—I'll touch you," Gertie threatened, lifting her hands up.

"You don't gross me out, Gertie." Bea leaned in close. "I already know how disgusting you are."

"L-lunch is going to be over in five minutes."

One of Bea's hands snapped forward and tried to yank down Gertie's skirt. Squealing, Gertie stumbled backward, her ass falling on the toilet seat. She held up her arms to deflect Bea's attack, but the girl snaked through the gap in her defense, gripping her hair and slamming it back against the dirty tile wall. Pain exploded in Gertie's head and she stifled a sob. With her free hand, Bea reached for the wall-mounted trash can. Unfortunately for Gertie, their lunch was the last of the day, which meant thing was filled to the brim with wilted tampon wrappers and other unmentionables. A sinking sense of dread washed over Gertie and she began to cry, but the louder she was, the harder Bea would wail on her.

While Bea clearly had the upper hand, there was something...off. Her expression was as hard as it ever was, but she kept gnawing on her lip, like she was nervous. Blood dripped down Gertie's sweaty forehead as she waited with bated breath for what Bea was about to say.

"Show me."

"Show you..." Gertie repeated, the words hot like

sparks against her tongue. "What are you talking about?"

"I just want to see it."

Her voice was unusually soft as she spoke—the tone of voice that Romeo would have used when calling to Juliet on her balcony. Bea brushed back a stray raven curl of Gertie's with an odd tenderness. But no matter how sweet a gesture, it made Gertie's stomach turn sour when she realized what Bea was *really* asking for.

"No," Gertie choked. "Let me out. Or I'll scream."

"Scream, and worse shit will happen," Bea snapped, then she lowered her voice again, coaxing her. "I won't touch it unless you want me to. I just want to see it."

"I'm on my *period,* Beatrice. Why would you…" Gertie stopped, realizing it was impossible to negotiate with a sociopath. She had to be careful when talking to Bea—she was nasty enough to willfully misinterpret things. She didn't want Bea to touch her, period or not. "You're fucking gross."

Bea's eyes widened with shock, wounded by Gertie's words. Malicious giggles erupted from her mouth. That softness left her posture and her gaze, and she cracked her neck in a sickening way. She reached for the receptacle again and thrusted her gloved hand inside, in which she grabbed a single blood-soaked tampon and held it high above her head. When she brought her reeking fist down, Gertie screamed for help, twisting her head from side to side. From her vantage point on the toilet seat, she couldn't get enough leverage to do any damage. Kicking did nothing but push her back against the stall door, and Bea would easily recover and come at her again. The stronger girl wrenched open her mouth and shoved the vulgar, steaming contents inside.

Gertie choked and sputtered as a rancid copper taste saturated her tongue, and her stomach pulsated violently in response. She vomited onto Bea, who screamed and stumbled backward out of the stall. On shaking knees, Gertie attempted to flee the restroom, sobbing and spitting the vile garbage from her mouth. Bea turned on the sink and tried to clean the puke off of her shirt.

"Hello?" A boy's voice shouted into the restroom. "Is everyone okay?"

"H-help," Gertie sobbed, army-crawling toward the exit. Her fingers scraped the discolored caulk between the floor tiles, thick and blubbery like steak gristle, as she dragged herself along. "Help me!"

For the longest time, Gertie had envisioned a white knight coming to her rescue, and amazingly, on the most traumatic of days, he arrived—Jack Burns, lanky, athletic, and sun kissed from too many afternoons playing soccer. He stumbled into the room and saw Gertie sprawled out across the floor, with a wide-eyed Bea hovering in the back, the bottom half of her puke-stained shirt soaked through.

Confused but determined, he rushed to Gertie's aid. The girl sobbed as he helped her to her feet, and it was only then that she realized how bruised she was from trying to fight off Bea's attacks. Frozen to her spot, Bea remained silent, scrubbing the same vomit stain over and over again. Through sobs and nasty belches, Gertie explained to her savior what had happened.

"It's not true," Bea snapped. "She's crazy."

Jack stared back in disgust. "Then why are you wearing gloves?"

Bea glanced at the damp plastic wrapped around her hands. She didn't respond. Jack called for help, and after what felt like forever, a few cafeteria attendants came to their aid.

The incident led to Bea's expulsion from the school, and in an odd twist of fate, the start of Gertie's romance with Jack. As a nerd, she had written off jocks as slovenly airheads, but when he accompanied her to the nurse's office that day, he challenged every preconceived notion she had. He listened to her cry about Bea's bullying, watched her wash the bile from her mouth, and held her hand while they waited for her dad to arrive. When she worked up the courage to return to school a few days later, he brought her the homework she'd missed and five fresh-cut daisies from his mother's garden—a miniature bouquet that signified his oath to keep what happened that day a secret, to spare her from further shame and humiliation.

# Chapter One

Middle school puppy love morphed into a high school courtship whose intensity rivaled that of Shakespearian romances, minus the chaos and bloodshed. Each day, Jack would walk Gertie to school and accompany her in between classes. After he got his license, they would drive everywhere together. They almost never had a destination in mind though. Long afternoons transformed into blissful midnights. They'd park somewhere in a clearing and lie in the bed of the truck so they could watch the stars. This was one thing Gertie didn't know much about, but Jack, who had gone camping with his grandfather when he was young, would tell her all about the constellations. Sometimes he'd tell the same stories over and over again, but she didn't mind. In a way it was kinda cool that she could recite the myth of Orion's Belt from memory.

When they weren't driving around or stargazing, Gertie was attending his practices and soccer games. He would always wave to her whenever their eyes met, but his friends didn't hide their disdain. They often scowled at her when Jack wasn't looking, and as sweet on her as he was, she was too afraid to ever tell him that his friends didn't like the fact he was dating a fat geek. But while Gertie was a coward, she wasn't a quitter. She was determined to remain the apple of Jack's eye by any means necessary. In her sophomore year, she joined the team as its manager, developed a strong rapport with the boys, and in little time, won their good graces. Her dedication to Jack's athletic career impressed all those within their circle. Even when she was juggling multiple AP classes, she would be copying new plays and snack lists for each of the boys. Turns out, she was great with strategy, at destroying the enemy.

Throughout all of this, Gertie learned not only about soccer, but about herself. With his constant presence, she rarely felt fearful when visiting the bathroom anymore, but just for safety purposes, he would wait outside. She never had to worry about returning to her father's cold and brutalist house, where the lights were always low and the furniture came in fifteen shades of black. She could go to Jack's house, hug his mother and inhale her cinnamon smell, and have long conversations with his father about music after dinner. When she was a small child, Gertie felt like a passenger, unable to control what direction she was heading in. But at least with him, the car wasn't empty.

By the end of his junior year, Jack had scored more goals than anyone in their high school's history. But his promising career was ruined when he tore his Achilles during a match. All the scouts lost interest. The fallout was terrible, but Gertie comforted him through all of it, further cementing her place as the apple in his ever-widening eyes. When his friends left him behind, and when the people that had looked at him with sparkling eyes fizzled out. No longer the athletic boy wonder, he became another nobody, and for Jack—an only child used to shining in the spotlight—that tore him apart. She'd glue the pieces back together, through gentle hugs and hand squeezes, through small love notes that she'd pass to him in between classes. For the possibility of a smile, she would try anything.

"But didn't I let you down?" he asked her one night, toward the end of one of their regular drives. "You used to have the trophy boyfriend."

"You were never a trophy for me, Jack. You were— are—my person. You still are."

It surprised no one when they got married three days after graduation. Gertie went to Penn to pursue a PoliSci degree, and Jack followed, picking up an apprenticeship in an auto shop and working to support them both. He had decided that since she'd spent so much of high school looking after him and helping him with his career, he would do the same in kind for her. She'd spend long nights poring over the textbooks spread out over their dining room table, and he would sit next to her, scribbling notes on flashcards for her to memorize on the bus. She never had to worry about cooking a single dinner, because by the time she got home, the cast iron would be on the stove, and the oven would be full of biscuits. He rarely made anything from scratch—with his hours at the shop, he could never find the time—but nothing had ever tasted as good to her as the frozen store-bought lasagna he'd have waiting for her on the table. After she graduated, they moved back to their hometown of Appledale to start the next stage of their life.

Gertie had thought the next stage would involve law school, but she hadn't counted on getting pregnant with June. Jack had lifted her off the ground bridal-style, and spun her around in a circle, overjoyed. His enthusiasm never faltered, not when the baby had torn Gertie from end to end, not when June developed colic, and not when the postpartum depression hit with the force of a semi-truck and she couldn't get out of bed. Even when she felt as though her madness had pushed him to his breaking point, he had loved her with a fierceness she knew she didn't deserve.

Time and time again, Gertie couldn't help but question how she had gotten so lucky. How had a woman like her, with a belly that always puffed over the edges of her pants like an overcooked cupcake, ever attracted such a charming, handsome, loving man? After long, wistful hours of pondering, she decided he was heaven-sent. Jack was an absolute angel; the universe's way of rewarding her for all those years of trauma and suffering at the indifference of her father and the vicious girls at school.

# Chapter Two

On the night of their sixth wedding anniversary, Jack treated Gertie to a candlelit dinner at a new Italian restaurant. The food had received rave reviews, but unbeknownst to the customers, management was absent minded, and had been improperly issued a few permits. Gertie never quite understood the details behind what happened—a bus boy broke a wine glass above the warming lamp their meals rested beneath, an overworked chef didn't bother to taste before it went out, the waitress had been distracted by something on her phone—it was not important.

Not as important as the discussion they were having that night.

"I think we need to get it out of the way now," he told her with a wry smirk, sipping from his glass of wine. "Think about it. We have the other baby *now*, we get our forties free to do whatever."

She giggled. "And what do you think we'll do?"

"Travel. Lots and lots of traveling." He poured more wine into her glass. "Picture this. A sailboat. The *S.S...Orion*. Sailing all over the Mediterranean. You spend your days lounging on the deck topless—"

"Jack Burns, why am I topless in this scenario?"

"Why wouldn't you be?"

"If I'm topless, then you're not wearing pants."

"You act like that's a punishment. Look, if you're not topless, how are you supposed to get an even tan?" He tapped his finger against his head. "I think of these things, Gert."

"All the important things." She laughed. It amazed her that after so many years together he could still make her crack up. She used her napkin to dab away some of the tears around her eyes, chuckling. "Okay, so your vision for our retirement is for me to lie around half naked on a boat all day."

"Hey, hey, hey! I'd take you places. Rome. Greece. *Monaco*. Ooh, bet you didn't know I knew where *that* one was."

"All this to say you think we should have another baby right now?"

His voice quieted. "I mean, if you were up for it. I know law school's on the horizon. And I know the first go-around was rough for you."

"Next time I'm getting a Cesarean."

"For sure." He reached across and squeezed her hand, his expression soft. "We can have another baby whenever we want. Or we don't have to."

"Oh gee, I don't know about that. Wouldn't want to wreck your dreams," she teased, but he didn't laugh.

He shook his head. "*This* is my dream, Gert. Every day I wake up, I'm living it."

She smiled, bashful. Averted her gaze and took another bite of her chicken parm. He smiled back, forked a large clump of salad, and chewed. Within seconds, he was choking, and when she realized he wasn't clearing it, she was on her feet, screeching for a waiter to come and help them, like that would make a difference. Most who swallow glass are torn apart from the inside out, the wounds not visible to the human eye, but for Jack—her beloved, angelic, too-good-for-this-world husband—one long, snaggly piece caught sideways in his throat, piercing a gaping hole just above his Adam's apple. Burgundy blood spurted out over his Caesar salad, coating it like a freshly made pasta sauce, before his head splatted into the bowl.

She had held his hand long after the warmth had left his body.

In the aftermath, her grief-stricken in-laws sued the restaurant and Appledale. The resulting payout was the largest in the city's history—a whopping 12.2 million dollars—the council members would grumble about for the next thirty years. After taxes, funeral costs, and lawyer fees, what remained was gifted to Gertie, now a 26-year-old widow with a tiny tot. This amount, coupled with the payout from his life insurance policy and a financial adviser who managed her investments, made her insanely rich.

For the first couple of years after his death, she was aimless. With so much money to her name, she had no need to work, and therefore, very little need to get out of bed aside from taking June to preschool and tending to her garden. At the encouragement of her mother-in-law, she did start seeing a therapist, but a therapist could not rescue her the way that Jack had. No matter how many people extended their hearts to her, Gertie felt painfully alone. At her core, she knew no one would love her the way he had, and she would never love anyone the way she'd loved him. Without him, life had no meaning, no rhythm, no light. Nothing could convince her otherwise, not even June.

What brought her out of her shell came in the form of a flier from her daughter's first grade teacher, desperately requesting assistance for an upcoming field trip. At the pleading of June, who wanted her mother to not be so emotionally comatose and absent from society, Gertie agreed to chaperone a group of ten kids to the zoo. When the teachers realized Gertie had no real commitments, they clung to her like sloths on trees.

*Mrs. Burns, I hate to trouble you, but could you help us with our class carnival?*

*We're hosting a fundraiser banquet for new playground equipment. Could you chip in?*

*Some of the kids need a little extra help reading... Would you be willing to help them practice?*

At first, Gertie had been absent minded in her efforts to help out her daughter's school. It was something to get her out of the house, and for whatever reason, it made June happy. But in time, Gertie noticed that the more she participated, the better June's opportunities. Somehow, she would be selected for student awards, given special access to gifted and talented programs, and received the best grades out of anyone in her class. After seeing her daughter achieve so much success, Gertie knew—she just knew—this was a result of her own brilliance. June was intelligent, sure, but she wasn't a go-getter. In Gertie's mind, opportunities were not handed to people, one had to work for them—or, someone had to work on your behalf. Beyond that, she realized that if she played an active role in her daughter's education, as opposed to what her father had done, she could ensure that she was protected. When June entered the second grade, Gertie joined the school's PTA. Later that year, she would be elected as president, and remained in that position until June finished elementary school.

# Chapter Three

Rumors about Gertie spread far and wide in their town.

*...That lovely lady, bless her soul. She's a widow, you know, and she dedicates all her time to helping others' children...*

*Mrs. Burns is truly an angel. Did you know that she keeps a spare leash and collar in her car so that she can rescue strays? I've heard that she's fostered five dogs...*

*...She raised the most money for the coat drive out of anyone,* ever. *She's brilliant.*

Just as June benefited from the attention, Gertie did as well. At the businesses owned by other PTA members, she enjoyed discounted meals and free products; during the holiday seasons she was awarded with lavish gifts and danced at parties she never imagined she would be invited to without Jack. The praise was to Gertie what cocaine was to a frat boy: intoxicating, adrenaline-filling, and essential for a good time.

She chased that high with an almost manic dedication, and with June excelling so much, Gertie began to set her sights higher. When June was in the sixth grade, she submitted an application to an elite charter school—Trinity Oaks—located in the wooded outskirts of town. The school had only been built ten years ago and boasted state of the art facilities—a 2,500 seat auditorium, MacBooks in every classroom, and even a nation-ranked fencing team. With Gertie's popularity around town, and some curated social media reminders about her dead husband, June would be a shoo-in.

However, this PTA was a little harder to climb. In public school, she was less likely to find involved parents, but the PTA for Trinity Oaks was full of women who'd peaked in high school, who clung to their meager duties with a desperation that Gertie found pitiful. They weren't as competent or as dedicated as she was, and it wasn't long until Gertie had cozied up to the existing president—a woman whose name she could never remember. Daisy? Donna? Dorothea? Oh yes, that was it, *Dorothea*. Too prissy for an ordinary Dorothy, she had to have the *thea*.

Early on, Gertie had sidled up to her and had performed the work of others; everything from decorating to budgeting to sending out invites for fundraising events. Despite Gertie's obvious desire to obtain total control, Dorothea was reluctant to relinquish her PTA title, and had politely declined to step out of the running for president when Gertie had suggested it to her.

"It's a lot of work, but I don't mind."

"I know, but you've had a lot on your plate this year," Gertie said. "What with your mother getting sick and all. And I thought that you said Todd wanted you to spend more time at home?"

"Oh, well—he just fusses. That's how men are when women have free time. You know how they are…"

When Dorothea trailed off, with her eyes lacking so much as an inkling of shame in saying this to a widow, she had sealed her fate in stone. That same day Gertie called an escort agency and hired a gorgeous brunette who would conveniently keep running into Dorothea's husband until the lonely asshole fell for her. She hired a P.I. to follow them on their meet ups, and six months later, a hefty manila folder full of spicy photographs landed in that stupid bitch's mailbox. Marriage ruined, PTA presidency secured.

From that experience, Gertie learned three things: first, it was easy to ruin someone's life if you had enough time and money. Second, she never had to get her hands dirty unless she wanted to. And third?

It was really fucking fun.

# Chapter Four

Another rabbit had gotten too comfortable among the plants of Gertie's herb garden. It was as brown as the bark on the trees, barely visible, if not for its fluffy white tail. She leaned on the pitchfork that she had been using to rearrange the mulch beds along the back fence, watching it hop onto the raised bed, its butt wiggling with excitement. In late fall, the rabbits were all too eager to fatten themselves up, and clearly, this little visitor thought he had hit the jackpot.

But he didn't count on the trap she had placed there.

A shrill squeal cut through the air as iron jaws closed around its midsection. It thrashed in place, rattling from side to side, squalling for help. Rolling her eyes, Gertie yanked the pitchfork from the earth and stalked over to the defenseless intruder. She hovered over it, watching as its blood soaked into the dirt below, so damp it was turning to mud. *Ugh.* When she bought the trap, she hadn't considered that this would happen. Could she and June eat from a herb garden stained with blood? Would that make them ill?

The rabbit's beady eye fixated on her, and it quaked in her gaze. With a heavy sigh, Gertie raised the pitchfork above her head, and brought it down on the animal's neck. In the stillness that followed, she stared at the blood spattered on the leaves of the rosemary and basil—like morning dew, glittering in the fading light of the overcast morning.

Perhaps it was best to start over.

"Mom, can we get takeout?"

Gertie looked up from her MacBook. June had just waltzed through the front door, red faced from walking up the steep hill to their house. Wisps of frizzy blond hair—the color courtesy of her father, the texture from her mother—framed either side of her glistening face.

"Well, if you're craving Indian, I think I've got a coupon for that somewhere."

"Whatever you want," June replied, carefully taking off her shoes and setting them on the mat so as not to smudge the hardwood floors. "Just as long as I don't have to do dishes tonight, I'm good. Big calc test tomorrow."

"Sounds good to me, sweetheart."

June flashed her an award-winning smile before

bounding up the stairs. Gertie closed her MacBook and set the device on the kitchen counter, then migrated over to the junk drawer where she kept all the takeout menus. After fumbling through them briefly she decided on Chinese takeout. June loved the pork spare ribs and orange chicken from here, and Gertie didn't mind a cream-cheese filled wonton or two. She called to place the order—the Wus ran the restaurant, and they knew her from her work with the PTA, so they offered her a friends and family discount—then set off to pick up the food.

Although it was almost twenty years old, Gertie still drove around in Jack's 2000 Ford pickup. Despite the fact that it was a gas guzzler, she could never bring herself to get rid of it. Plus, she had a ton of great memories in this car. They had sex for the first time in the backseat while listening to Bob Seger's *We Got Tonight.*

*Hmm.* That sounded like a nice song to listen to, on a beautiful late afternoon such as this. Orange sunlight, creamy and rich like a dreamsicle, streamed through the interlocking branches of trees that rested below the horizon in the distance. She drove slowly, singing along to the song and drumming her fingertips against the wheel.

The Chinese restaurant was a fifteen-minute drive from where she lived, but thanks to traffic and construction along the main roads, it took her about twenty-five. Gertie pulled into the parking lot, avoiding the people that were hauling across their laundry from the dry cleaner next door. She pulled into a spot toward the front, and hopped out of the car. The sunlight was sinking lower, and the night was growing colder. When she breathed, a small fog left her mouth. She grumbled underneath her breath for not having brought a jacket, but in truth, she didn't mind it too much. This was June's junior year. There would only be so many times left where she would be getting her food, and afterwards—

—well, she wasn't ready to think about that.

Shivering, she shuffled her way inside the building, and heaved a sigh of relief. Thanks to the open-air kitchen, this place was almost always sweltering. She unbuttoned her cardigan and shuffled to the back of the room, behind another woman with cropped blond hair who was arguing with Mrs. Wu. Probably about some sort of online order issue or something. Gertie rolled her eyes. In recent years, the Wus only had a functioning website on the rare occasions when their son Michael was home from college.

The woman reached into her purse and pulled out her threadbare wallet. She dumped out all her cards, unzipped the side pocket, and poured an ocean of coins onto the countertop. Mrs. Wu muttered something in Mandarin, frown lines betraying her calm demeanor—she was fed up with the bullshit; another white woman babbling about whatever.

Gertie checked the time on her phone. *Ugh.* Her food was probably cold by now. *What is this lady's problem?* She watched as the woman desperately tried to count out different coins, laughing like a nervous hyena the whole time. Irritating. Who had the audacity to pay for something in coins? Mrs. Wu was far too polite to turn away business, so when it became clear the woman wasn't leaving, Gertie cleared her throat and approached.

"Hey," Gertie said. "Is your card not working? If so, I've got it."

The woman shook her head dismissively, not bothering to look up. "No, no, I've got it. Just a second. Thank you."

"Really." Gertie withdrew her credit card and passed it to Mrs. Wu. "Whatever she ordered, can you just put it on my card?"

Mrs. Wu smiled. "How generous."

*Not really*, Gertie thought to herself, but she smiled back regardless. She needed to get home to June, and besides, as a multi-millionaire, it wasn't a big deal to pay for others' food. She had spent far more expensive sums on charity galas and ruining the lives of her competitors. The cash register burped out her receipt and Gertie signed it. The woman didn't say anything the entire time, just stood beside her, stiff with a slight upturn in her lip. Gertie thought nothing of it—maybe she was too prideful to thank her. She knew the type.

"Gertie? Gertie Taylor?"

Gertie froze at the mention of her maiden name. She slowly turned to look at the woman, who beamed at her with a familiarity she didn't understand. The woman was pretty, around her age. Crow's feet at the corners of her eyes, laugh lines around her mouth, but otherwise envious skin. For a brief moment Gertie wondered if that's what her skin would look like if she'd invested in more retinol products in her twenties.

"Do you recognize me?" the woman asked with a coy smile. "I don't blame you if you don't. But my God, you look—you look the same! Just the same, but just as good."

"Did we meet at a banquet for Trinity Oaks?"

"Trinity Oaks—isn't that the charter school?" The woman shook her head, chuckling. "No. I'm—I'm Beatrice. Beatrice Robinson."

"Beatr—" Gertie stopped herself.

She blinked and turned back to Mrs. Wu to accept her grease-stained brown bag. The smile faded from Bea's face as Mrs. Wu's eyes shifted between them, aware of the tension but unsure of what to say.

"You're welcome for the food," Gertie mumbled as she brushed past.

Beatrice. *Bea.* Why hadn't she recognized her? She looked almost the same as she had in junior high, just with shorter hair. When Bea was expelled, they had lost touch—no more Carrie-inspired bathroom encounters, only the nightmares that stayed with her. Besides, Gertie wasn't the type to check up on her nemeses, unless she wanted something from them. She didn't social-media stalk people; she blocked them. Out of sight, out of mind. Well, now Bea had fallen within her line of sight again, residual trauma bubbling within her like an over-shaken soda can.

"Gertrude!"

Gertie turned back to face Bea, who stood on the sidewalk with a desperate expression, cradling her bag of takeout close to her chest. She crossed the street to her, and for some reason, Gertie didn't run. She felt frozen, bewitched to the spot, and from that, she felt a deep sense of shame. All these years, and this girl still held so much power over her.

Bea smiled, sheepish. "Hi. The lady inside told me that you go by Mrs. Burns now. Not Taylor. My bad."

Gertie arched her brow, but didn't say anything. She appraised Bea once more, taking in her outfit. Clearly thrifted items, judging from the shoddy stitching job along the elbows and wrists of her plaid shirt. Joggers that appeared to have barbecue-sauce stains on them. But damn, beneath the sloven outfit, Bea's body was tight. *Ugh.* Gertie was even curvier than she was as a child; her hips had spread a little wider, her ass hung a little lower. Jack had found her body beautiful, but she never understood why, especially when she looked at women like Bea. What she wouldn't give to feel both powerful *and* beautiful. She would be unstoppable. But even though she loathed her body, she loathed the plastic-y look of a manufactured body even more.

Bea's smile faltered at Gertie's heated silence. "Um…
thank you. I appreciate it. My youngest was getting tired of
Kraft mac, and y'know, so was I. I can pay you back."

"There's no need for that." *Truly, no need.* Bea must've
been out of the loop. Where had she been all these years?

"Really, I can do it. I don't like taking handouts. If
you've got a Venmo, I can pay you back when I get my next
check."

"No." Gertie jingled her keys and unlocked her car,
slowly inching her way toward it. "I'm good."

"If you insist." But Bea didn't move. She stared at Gertie as she set the bag of food in the passenger seat of her car.
"It's good to see you. Have you been in Appledale all these
years?"

"Most of them." Gertie slammed the door shut.

"Ahh. See, uh, I got a divorce, I'm staying with my
parents…it's a whole thing. It's good to see an old friend."

Gertie spun her head around so hard, she thought it
would snap off. *Friend?* They had never been friends. *What is
she going on about?* Bea bit her lip and switched the bag to her
other hand. She scraped her shoe against the asphalt, like she
had stepped in dog shit and needed to clean it off.

"I know," Bea assured her. "I shouldn't be calling you
that."

"We were never friends."

"I know, I know."

29

"You…" *This is stupid.* She wasn't still hung up on what had happened in middle school. She was a powerful woman now, and powerful women didn't wallow in the sadness of their trauma—they found a way to profit from it. But there was nothing about this situation that she could construe to her benefit. "You know what, it's fine. I should be getting home. My daughter's waiting for me."

"You have a daughter. Wow," Bea breathed. Gertie frowned, trying to discern what her expression meant. Heavy lids, rosy cheeks, glossy eyes. It felt familiar in an ugly way. "Time really flies, I guess."

"I have to go home," Gertie reiterated, irritation taut in her voice. Bea was taken aback for a moment. Gertie sighed, dragging a hand through her hair. "Sorry. Tired. I just gotta get home."

Bea shuffled in place. "I don't blame you for feeling the way that you do. I was horrible to you."

*You nearly sexually assaulted me in a bathroom,* Gertie thought to herself, pissed. Well, she didn't know what Bea had wanted from her that day. She had asked Gertie to show her vulva, and had offered to touch it for some reason. Maybe Bea wouldn't have forced herself upon Gertie. Then again, maybe there was another reason why Bea had brought a pair of plastic gloves with her. The memory made her squeamish, and the fact that Bea was standing here so casually offended her, right down to her core.

"I owe you an apology, and I owe you for food," Bea said. "Look, um..." She set her bag on top of a Subaru Outback, then fished in her pocket for her phone. "Why don't you give me your number, and I'll give you mine."

"An apology?"

"You know. For years of terrorizing you. And for... that day. The incident. You know what? You have to go, let me stop talking. Here's my number." Bea offered her phone with shaking hands. "C-can you give me yours?"

Gertie rolled her eyes and snatched the phone from Bea. She could always just block her. It didn't matter. Bea wasn't a threat to her now. She didn't hold any of the menacing aura she had when they were kids. It was almost disappointing.

Almost.

"Thanks," Bea said, taking her phone back. "Want to have coffee sometime?"

"I'm pretty busy."

"Coffee," Bea insisted. "Least I can do. I'd—I'd love to catch up."

Gertie didn't say anything. Didn't so much as nod or shake her head. She climbed into her truck and left Bea to stand in the parking lot with that crestfallen expression, like a jilted bride left at the altar. Her mind was blank with fury as she drove home a little too aggressive, a little too fast. When she pulled into the driveway, she didn't remember how she got there.

With a huff and a shake of her head, she grabbed the bag of food and entered the house, her knees almost popping as she crept up the stone steps. At the sound of her mother coming through the door, June bounded down the stairs to set the table. Gertie didn't enjoy a single bite of food, and could hardly be bothered to entertain her daughter's attempts at conversation. She kept thinking of Bea, standing in that parking lot. Inviting her for coffee.

*How stupid. Pathetic, actually.*

Gertie didn't give her other childhood bullies the time of day either. There was no sense in repairing a burned bridge that only led to scorched earth.

Especially when Bea wouldn't be useful to her. *What obtuse jackass ordered takeout and tried to pay for it with coins?*

"Mom? You okay?"

Gertie smiled. "A little tired."

"Oh, okay." June pushed around some of the wilted peas from her fried rice. She still didn't like when certain foods touched. "Can we go shopping for my homecoming dress soon?"

"When do you want to go?"

"This weekend. Since it's my junior year, I wanted to go all out."

"Bling?"

"Ew," June said, wrinkling her nose. "I hate those kinds

of dresses. Rhinestones and sequins are so tacky. Well, sequins aren't that bad, but I would projectile vomit if I was wearing something with fake jewels and rhinestones stapled all over it. They literally look like a kindergartener's art project."

"Okay, okay," Gertie said, laughing. "What were you thinking?"

"Ballgown."

"For homecoming? I'd save that for prom."

"Oooh. Maybe you're right."

"Homecoming is less about taking fancy pictures than prom is. You want to have fun dancing with your friends. Maybe something short instead?"

"I'll think about it."

Gertie smiled, deep in thought. "A ballgown…I wore that to my first prom with your father."

"And on your wedding day."

"I loved that dress." She took a sip from her glass of water, suddenly feeling parched. "We'll go Saturday, after you're done with cheer."

It hadn't even been three hours, when Bea assaulted Gertie with a barrage of text messages. She was in the middle of heating up a bag of popcorn and getting ready to watch the latest season of *White Lotus*.

**BEA**

*What does Wednesday look like for you?*
*There's this place called Jack and the Bean*
*Like a play on "Jack and the Beanstalk" or something*
*Hahahaha*

Who, in this day and age, *actually* wrote out their laughter over text? Cringe. Gertie set her phone down on the console table and tried to refocus her attention on the show. But Bea continued to message her.

**BEA**

*If Wednesday doesn't work then Thursday is open for me*

One thing was certain: Bea was just as persistent as she had been as a child. Dedicated to annoying Gertie as if it was a fine craft. At this point, even if she blocked her, Bea would probably find some way to track her down like a bloodhound sniffing a foxhole. Even more frustrating though—

—Gertie was curious.

Perhaps she was gleeful at the idea of witnessing how far her nemesis had fallen, or maybe she was really fucking bored. After all, it had been a number of years since she'd run into any challenges with the PTA at Trinity Oaks, sans that passive aggressive bitch Misty, who always had a snide remark about something. Maybe now that Gertie knew who she was, she would enjoy watching her scrounge for change like some little Cockney leper in a Charles Dickens story.

That Wednesday she dressed in her finest—a button-up blouse that hugged the curves of her breasts, unbuttoned just enough to show cleavage, and a nice pair of high-waisted jeans. She showed up at the coffee shop ten minutes late, long enough to make Bea worry about whether she would show. After walking through an unkempt garden full of entangled vines and improperly maintained ivy trellises, she entered the restaurant and found Bea sitting at the back, close to a fireplace. She had cleaned up a bit from their meet-up at a Chinese restaurant, and wore tight, black pants, combat boots, and a plaid shirt with the sleeves rolled up high enough to reveal the collection of stick-and-poke tattoos along her biceps. Bea waved to her, and they grabbed their drink orders before returning to their seats.

"Thanks for making the time to meet with me," Bea said, chair scraping against the stone floor. "I hope the drive over wasn't too bad?"

"No. But making my way through that garden was."

"It's...certainly an interesting choice of theme." Bea tilted her head back to stare at the collection of fairytale books hanging on fishing wire from the ceiling. The musk of aged paper permeated the shop, overpowering the smell of the coffee beans pulsing away in industrial grinders. "I would've done *The Princess and the Bean*. Like *The Princess and the Pea*."

"And filled the space with mattresses?"

Bea chuckled. "People could take their pick. Sleep on a mattress, or have a Frappuccino."

"Hmm. Probably needs to be workshopped more before you bring it to an investor."

"Like I could ever be a business owner. Could barely pass remedial algebra." Bea played with the two sugar packets she'd snagged from the condiment dispensary. "So...uh, like I told you...I owe you an apology."

"You said that."

"Yeah. Um, I'm really embarrassed about it, to this day. I've been thinking over and over about what I would tell you, but I could never come up with the right words, because the truth of it is that it was completely fucked. *I* was completely fucked up. Uh..." Bea's hands trembled. "So I met with the principal that day, along with my parents and the school's officer. And—they asked me *why* I had done what I did, where I had learned it from..."

"And?"

"I told them the truth. From...um..." Bea's voice broke a little. "From my uncle."

Gertie fought the urge to recoil in shock, and bit down on her tongue instead. The taste of warm copper filled her mouth and she had to sip her coffee to get it down.

"So, that was a thing," Bea sighed. "After that I had to change schools."

"You mean you weren't expelled? That's what they told me."

"N-no. I mean, I probably would've been if I stayed. But at that point, I didn't...I didn't want anyone to find out about what I had told them. My uncle was arrested, and that was going to end up in the papers. I didn't want to show my face around there anymore."

"Oh."

"I did those things to you because I was trying to make sense of the things I had been taught by my uncle. And at the time, I was also struggling with my...my sexuality." Bea laughed a little too hard, and she gnawed on her chapped lips for a moment, frustrated. "I mean, clearly. *Clearly* that's been a running theme in my life, since I'm now divorced with two kids."

"Oh, so you recently..."

"Came out. Yes. That's what led to my divorce, and moving in with my parents. Well, actually, there's a lot more to the divorce, but the short answer is that I finally came out."

Gertie wasn't quite sure where this conversation was going. Where was the apology? The admission of wrongdoing? The pleading for forgiveness? If Bea had an ounce of humility or shame—as she claimed to have—surely she would've broken down by now. Pale-faced and big-eyed but no tears, no hoarseness in her throat.

"So...I did those things to you because I had a twisted

sense of what was appropriate."

"And it's always easy to pick on the weird girl."

"I didn't pick on you because you were weird. I did it because I liked you." Redness filled Bea's cheeks, and she averted her eyes, clearly ashamed. "I *really* liked you."

At this admission, a sharp breath escaped Gertie's chest. *What?* There was no way. Bea had liked her? Out of all the other girls in their class? Girls who were prettier and thinner and had nicer hair? Well, wasn't that just an unexpected, convenient explanation to everything that happened between them over the years? A piss poor one.

Gertie pushed her glasses up her nose. "You didn't like me. You hated me."

"I-I didn't," Bea protested gently. "I hated the feelings that you gave me, maybe, but I didn't hate you. I just didn't know how to deal with my shit back then."

Gertie leaned back in her seat, appalled. "That sounds like an excuse."

"It's not an excuse, it's a reason."

"If it's not an excuse, why bring it up?"

Bea flinched. She considered this, biting her lip. "I… You're right. I thought that you having the full context would help. But I guess it doesn't erase what I did."

*She guessed?* What a crock of bullshit. Twenty-some years since they had last seen each other, and this was the best Bea could come up with? Some sad-ass story about being molested by her uncle and how that lead to her having a twisted sense of desire? She didn't remember Bea being this stupid, although her comment about remedial algebra was certainly ringing a bell. Fuck this lady, having the nerve to traumatize her and then make herself out to be the victim. See, this was the thing with people who wronged you. They never want to apologize for the sake of *your* feelings; they only want to do it for themselves. This wasn't even an apology, actually. Bea never uttered the words, "I'm sorry." Effectively, she had wasted both of their time.

"Well," Gertie said politely, "thanks for coming clean, I guess. I always wondered why things had been the way they were. I think you're very brave to tell me this."

A blatant lie, but Bea was too dumb to understand that. Or was it—wait a minute.

Why was this woman blushing at her?

She couldn't be—

—*no?*—

—oh, but she was. That cheeky grin and those rosy cheeks said it all. Bea couldn't even look her in the eyes. Still? After all these years, this woman was in love with her?

How pathetic. *Delicious.*

Gertie folded her arms across the table and pushed them together to subtly squeeze her breasts up. She leaned forward ever so slightly and watched as Bea pulled away, avoiding eye contact. She wanted to laugh. Twenty years and the tables had turned drastically.

Gertie had all the power to ruin her life now.

Inside her head, the gears began to turn. Faster, faster, faster, it felt so good. She hadn't encountered a challenge like this in so long. Since she took over the presidency of the PTA, only three women had run against her, and it was easy to get her P.I. to dig up dirt against them. They were ruined before they even started their campaigns. But she already knew *all* the dirt on Bea, didn't need to drop hundreds of dollars to do it. It would be so easy to take advantage of this woman and demolish her as she had once tried to do to her so long ago. To dominate her and humiliate her in a way that pushed her to the brink of taking her own life, as Gertie had once done when she was far too young.

Hell, she might string the bitch up herself if the time was right.

*But how to play this?* "You haven't changed a bit, Bea. I can't believe I didn't recognize you at first. You look good."

Her blush spread to the tips of her ears. "You think so? I-I think you look better."

"Oh no." Gertie waved her hand dismissively, chuckling.

"No, I mean it," Bea said, nodding sincerely. Her eyes skimmed over her voluptuous body, and Gertie felt violated, but in a sickening way, also vindicated. "You walked through that door and my jaw almost dropped."

"Oh stop. I need to lose weight."

"I don't think so. I think you've got the weight in all the right places."

*Wow.* This dumbass had taken the bait so easily. She still felt like pouring acid into her eyes at the way that Bea looked at her, but she was giddy at how easy this was. Her mind flashed back to that day in the restroom, when her hands had gripped onto her hair, and how Bea's glove, damp with menstrual blood, had inched closer to her face. It didn't take much effort for her to remember the stench, like rotting eggs and vaginal sweat. She could fight through her disgust toward Bea if it meant taking her down.

"Gertie...is it me, or is there a crazy energy between us?" Bea murmured. Her hand slid across the table to hold hers. "I've felt like that since seeing you at the restaurant, at least."

"Bold," Gertie commented, staring at her captive hand.

Bea shrank back. "Sorry. I didn't mean to be forward." She froze, eyes wide open. "Wait. Your—your last name. Did you—are you—"

"—I'm a widow," Gertie explained. "I married Jack Burns."

"Jack, from...oh," Bea said, realizing. "I'm so sorry."

"N-no. Don't apologize," Gertie mumbled. This time, she reached for Bea's hand. It felt unnaturally cold and clammy, like a snake that had been submerged in ice water. "Look, I…I feel that way, too."

"Are you…queer?"

"I don't use labels." A lie disguised as a truth. She never had to use them, after all. "I don't date much, honestly. My daughter is my number one priority."

"Your daughter. Right. What's her name?"

"June."

"June. So nice." Bea's thumb stroked the top of her hand. It felt familiar.

"We wanted to name her after the goddess Juno, but everyone told us they'd just associate her with the pregnant teen from that film."

Bea laughed. "I would've."

"That name is permanently ruined." A smile tugged at the corner of Gertie's lips, this time a genuine one. "Since she was born in the winter, we thought it would be fun to name her after a summery month."

"Like she was your little summer oasis in the winter's cold," Bea said. "I love that."

Gertie learned that Bea worked as a stock clerk at the grocery store, which explained her toned muscles. She also learned about Bea's boys, Trevor and River. Trevor was around June's age. River had just started middle school. When Bea spoke about Trevor, she seemed hesitant, but she was more open about River, who she had nothing but praise for. If Bea didn't want to talk about Trevor, that meant he was a shitty kid. Gertie filed this tidbit inside her mental cabinet of useful information as they continued to chat and flirt for the next three hours.

At the end, Bea walked her to her car and Gertie invited her over for dinner that Friday. They hesitated there, hovering by the driver-side door of Jack's pickup, Bea's body quivering with excitement but still so nervous. She wanted to kiss her goodbye. Gertie knew. But Bea chickened out, instead squeezing her hand and bidding her goodnight.

When Gertie got home, she told her daughter to order a pizza for dinner, not caring that it had been the second time that week they'd eaten takeout. She locked herself in the master bathroom and reached underneath the sink for the small bottle of bleach she stored beneath it. She turned on the hot water, poured the liquid over her hands, and scrubbed vigorously until droplets of blood emerged from every crevice and callus on her skin. Layers of ivory flesh peeled back to reveal blotchy red beneath. Yet she still didn't feel clean.

Touching Bea was like reliving her worst nightmare all over again.

Wincing, she shut off the piping hot water and gently wrapped her hands up in a fluffy bath towel. Apple-blossom pink spots emerged on the surface moments later. Agony, which had delayed itself in her manic episode, settled in. She hissed cuss words between clenched teeth.

At least she could sit and writhe in silence without June bothering her. June already knew about her bizarre bathroom habits, and knew not to question her if she took an extraordinary amount of time. Inside her purse, her phone buzzed, and she flinched at the sound, dreading seeing Bea's name. But no, not Bea.

Misty. Asking about the budget for the Parents' Night party.

*Shit.*

She had been so distracted this week that she forgot to work on all the things she'd normally do. If taking Bea down was going to preoccupy so much of her mind, then she had to make sure the takedown was worth it.

*Brainstorm. How would you take down your arch nemesis? How had Brutus slain Caesar? No.* No. *This would not be as clean as* Julius Caesar. Bea didn't deserve as clean and neat a finale. This was more of a *Mean Girls* scenario, but gayer. Except this time, Cady Heron wasn't *becoming* Regina George, she would be fucking her, and instead of hitting her with a bus, she would shatter her heart so horrifically that the bitch would OD on some ibuprofen and die.

Gertie thought of her own life. What would it take for her to be ruined? Financial loss—that was one. Losing her house. Losing Jack's car. June's college fund. But Bea didn't have oodles of cash, and she didn't have a job that paid well enough that it would matter if she lost it.

*Lose.* Losing personal items. Something precious. Everyone had something that meant a lot to them. *Bea's kids. Could I do that? Could I take them away? A phone call to child protective services...no.* That was a different kind of cruelty. Gertie could figure something else out. What else did she know? Divorcée with a questionable ex-husband and an even more questionable son. Back to the family. Support system. *Bea's living with her parents. They were on the chopping block, too.* Add a romance of a lifetime with a traumatic, painful end, and Gertie was *certain* she could pull this off. She'd dress in the brightest of blacks for Bea's funeral and wear one of those fishnet veils so no one could see her smile.

    She was going to rewrite the rulebook on how to play revenge.

# Chapter Five

The hallowed halls of Trinity Oaks always felt drafty, but today was particularly painful. As Gertie walked up the stone steps into the school, laptop bag in hand, she zipped up her coat further, until the folds of it almost swallowed her chin. Thursdays were PTA meeting nights, and also when June was at rehearsal for the fall musical. Tonight's discussion was about the annual Parents' Night event, which would be held in exactly two weeks.

Gertie fake-smiled at her daughter's teachers when she passed them in the hallways, and migrated through the throngs of students that were beginning to leave their final classes. The FACS classroom (or "Home Ec," but Trinity was too posh for such a term) on the east side was where their meetings were hosted, as it was scarcely used due to low enrollment. Always the first to arrive, Gertie flicked on the lights, unpacked her canvas bag full of crunchy vegetable straws, and opened her laptop to the budget. She greeted each member of the PTA as they entered the room: Misty Brightly, the bitchy one; Joanna Lewinski, whose twin boys played basketball; Kellyanne Cunningham, who talked like she had three caffeinated drinks in her system at any given time; and their designated teacher "chaperone", the bookish Norah Nguyen.

"Ladies," Kellyanne said, excited, "did you hear that a position opened up on the school board?"

"Oh my god, *yes*." Misty laughed.

"The school board?" Gertie echoed. "No, I had not."

"Really?" Misty said, casting her eyes around at the others. Never meeting Gertie's eyes. "I would've thought you'd be the first to know."

Gertie ignored the obvious dig. "So what happened?"

"Well," Misty said, batting her eyelashes, "turns out that Wendy Hsu was convicted of a"—she lowered her voice to a conspiratorial whisper—"DUI on Friday night. Which is—"

"—a felony!"

"And so she resigned this morning before they could force her to. Can you imagine? I've spoken to the woman so many times at board meetings and yet, I never thought she was a drunk."

"Goodness. Was anyone hurt?" Norah asked gently.

"Aside from a mailbox and—wait, nope, she definitely killed someone's dog. Flattened the poor thing right in front of a little girl, from what I've heard."

Norah touched her heart to her chest, unable to speak. Joanna, a mom to two rescue Beagles, covered her mouth with her hands. Gertie grimaced. If anyone had caused that sort of trauma to June, they wouldn't be so lucky to get away with a DUI.

"They're going to hold a special election in March, Gertie," Kellyanne said. "I think you should run for it."

"But Gertie's busy with the PTA," Misty protested, laughing. She cast a wayward glance in Gertie's direction. "Unless she's willing to relinquish the throne."

"Well…"

The idea of being on a school board, which would have power to enact tangible change, *did* seem appealing to her. Especially since June was graduating from school in a couple of years, and if she had to deal with Misty nagging her for a budget one more time, she just might shove the woman's head inside a blender and press pulse until she could make a pulpy juice from that wilted thing she called a brain.

She wouldn't ever actually do that, though, even if her stomach gurgled at the thought. It was simply an idea she entertained from time to time.

Gertie responded to Kellyanne's suggestion with an, "I don't know, I guess we'll see," and then proceeded with the rest of the meeting. She provided Misty with her budget and delegated tasks to the remaining members. Overall, the discussions went slow—brutally slow—but that was normal the closer they got to the event. After it ended, Gertie collected June from the auditorium, and they drove home. Not less than five minutes from the school, Gertie's phone buzzed.

She rolled her eyes. Probably Misty again. "Grab that, will you?"

"Sure thing." June's surprised eyes and wrinkled nose communicated that it was, in fact, *not* Misty. "Who is Bea?"

"Bea?" Gertie clenched the steering wheel tighter.

"You're getting dinner with her this Friday?"

"Oh—well, she's coming over. She's an old friend."

June giggled. "Didn't know you had friends, Mom."

"What? I have tons of friends."

"You have PTA members."

"Friends. Whatever. I have a social life. Better than Vicky Brightly's mother. Her only friends are her AA sponsors."

June recoiled, shocked by her mother's vicious dig. Her lower lip protruded in a childlike pout and she turned to look out the window. "That's not very nice."

"No, it's not, but neither was your comment." She exhaled, slow and careful, her mouth forming a perfect puckered "O." *Calm down, Gertrude. You don't want to do this. She's a teenage girl.*

This was Bea's presence at work again. It was malevolent—poisonous, like cancer. First she had forgotten about the budget, now she was snapping at her perfect, albeit some-what bitchy, daughter.

"I'm sorry." She reached one hand over to squeeze June's knee. "Been a stressful day."

June's pouty expression deflated somewhat. "Misty again?"

"When isn't it Misty?" Gertie laughed. "But actually, I learned about this school board position opening up and I was thinking I should run."

"Do it! That sounds like fun."

"Y'know, I don't know. Running for a political posi-tion is a lot of work, and it's your junior year…you have all these big events coming up."

June snorted. "It wouldn't be forever."

"No, but…" Gertie glanced over at her daughter, who had perked up. "You really think I should do it?"

"Yes! You don't need my permission. Go for it."

Perfect like her father. Gertie smiled. "Thanks, Junebug."

"So tell me more about Bea. Is she a friend from Penn or something?"

"Uh, no. From elementary school." Gertie cleared her throat as she pulled into the driveway. "Honey, can you grab the mail before coming inside?"

Gertie dodged her overly curious daughter's questions about Bea until Friday rolled around, when—*Thank Christ*—she had a homecoming game to cheer for, and she had the house to herself. She decided to go simple but upscale. Rib eyes (she knew Bea was not one of those vegan gays, thank God) paired with smashed potatoes alongside roasted carrots mixed with goat cheese crumbles. Bea arrived with a bottle of wine and a bouquet of flowers shortly after 7 p.m. She wore a sports coat, and her gel-laden hair was plastered against her skull. When she stepped inside, Gertie could smell the hibiscus wafting off of it.

She accepted the flowers from Bea and smiled. "Thank you. These are lovely."

"I brought over a rosé. Couldn't decide between red or white."

"Aw, you didn't have to do that." *No, really, Bea did* not *have to do that.*

This woman literally couldn't even pay for takeout, and she was off spending money on *wine?* And fresh flowers? Flowers that looked like they didn't come from the grocery store? They were tied with a lace bow and there were—

—daisies.

Exactly five.

"Gertie?"

She shook her head. "I love daisies. They're my favor-ite."

"Oh! Wow, I didn't even know that. You mentioned at the coffee shop that you liked gardening, so I-I thought I'd bring you flowers," Bea stammered. "Although you didn't mention how *big* of a garden you had, so I guess my gift pales in comparison."

*Oh. Right.* She hadn't prepared her for that. Gertie lived on the outskirts of Appledale, in a two-story French country home that sat on five acres of wooded land. She had bought the house a couple of years after Jack's death. While Gertie lived modestly, her house—and the accompanying gar-den, straight out of a cottagecore Pinterest board—was any-thing but.

"It's gorgeous, but I didn't realize how well-off you were. I feel almost embarrassed. No wonder you paid for my meal."

"And no wonder I didn't want you to pay me back."

Bea giggled.

Gertie felt strange. She turned away from Bea and wandered into the kitchen to find a vase for the flowers, Bea traipsing after her. The steaks were sizzling in the cast-iron skillet in the oven, and the smashed potatoes were cooling on the counter.

"Wow, this smells *incredible*."

Bea set the bottle of wine on the counter and Gertie fetched a cork to pop it open. After pouring a couple of glasses, she checked inside the oven and pulled out the steaks. Creamy butter bubbled and foamed atop the juicy hunks of meat and garlic. She placed them on a plate to rest and offered her a seat at the kitchen table. As they waited, they chatted over mundane aspects of their everyday—River had already found a new pair of bullies at school, Trevor was being a shit, Bea's parents were verbally abusing her. In a way, Gertie felt like she was playing therapist, and the very thought made her want to drink all the wine and bash Bea's head open with the bottle. Somehow, she resisted the urge. When Bea asked about her own life, she admitted she had submitted her application to run for the school board.

"The school board?" Bea crowed, eyes wide. "So you're running for a political office?"

Gertie was surprised that Bea was intelligent enough to grasp that it was—technically—a political position. "Yes. I think I mentioned during our coffee date that I was on the PTA. Well, once June graduates from school, I won't be able to serve on the PTA anymore, and I thought it would be a good change of pace."

"I bet. And you leave a good impression on people. You're a shoo-in."

Flattered, Gertie smiled. Bea raised her glass and made a toast to her candidacy and new beginnings. Pleasant conversation, aided by cheap wine, continued throughout dinner. Once they finished, they migrated to the living room and curled up on the couch with their wine glasses freshly replenished.

Bea was giggly, her eyes glassy like moonstones. "You're spoiling me," she said.

"I wanted to make our first official date special."

"Well, you've more than succeeded. But I can think of another way to make it special."

Bea set down her glass, and immediately Gertie stiffened. Was it too late to kill this woman and bury her outside, perhaps underneath the hydrangeas? Could someone this skinny and tall be a decent meal for her precious plants? Thoughts of violence swam through Gertie's mind as Bea leaned over and cupped her face in her hands. The kiss was soft and sweet, but Gertie couldn't help but shudder.

Bea swiped her tongue across her lips, her eyelids lowering, voice soft as she spoke. "That's the biggest reaction I've ever gotten from a kiss."

"Y-you're really good at it."

Gertie responded, breathless, her hatred bubbling inside her like a painful bout of heartburn. But her expression must not have betrayed her words, because Bea leaned in for another one. She knew she couldn't be so stiff, she had to sell it. She wove her fingers in Bea's greasy hair and suppressed the urge to gag, her mouth pushing back against Bea's with a feverish urgency. Bea's hands dropped from her face, and she made a noise that sounded like a cross between a moan and a whimper.

*Right.* Gertie didn't have to be subjected to this like some damsel in distress. She could take the lead. She could be the...top? Is that the term, or is that just for gay men? *Oh, who cares.*

She pressed Bea down against the sofa and planted soft kisses along her neck, hoping that would clean the taste of her from her mouth. Instead, all she could taste was salted skin and vague, bitter traces of cheap cologne. Bea giggled and moaned and responded with favor to her touch, oblivious to Gertie's growing frustration. After ten minutes of planting kisses on her lips, neck, and collarbone, she was undone by her impatience. There *had* to be a way to hurry this process along—this was never an issue with Jack.

Continuing to kiss Bea, Gertie's hand, slow and purposeful, traced the space between her breasts. For a moment, she wished she had claws so she could enact some serious damage. Dig, dig, dig into her flesh and rip out that fatty heart. Her hand drew a line down the center of her body, splitting it into two symmetrical parts. As Bea writhed at her touch, she fantasized about her body unzipping, the guts unspooling like thread from a roll of yarn, the blood staining the white sofa until it was irrevocably ruined.

Then her hand slipped below the waistline of Bea's

pants, and the spell was broken. She sat up, eyes wide, perfectly sober.

"What's wrong?" Gertie asked.

"I just..." Bea bit her lip. "I don't think we're...ready."

"O-oh." Gertie sat back, confused.

"I'm so sorry. My last girlfriend—she was—fuck, I'm sorry." Bea pressed her wrists against her eyes, huffing in exasperation. "You're gonna hate me."

"Try me."

Bea blinked, shocked by Gertie's serious tone. Once again, she interpreted her behavior as earnestness, not irritation. Bea hugged one of the throw pillows to her chest and scooted away from her a tad, as if afraid of physical retaliation.

"So...my divorce was messy. Messy for many, *many* reasons. My hus—my ex-husband, Westley, is not a good guy. When I was in the closet, I was trying to forget about my attraction to women, but..."

Over the course of a long twenty minutes, Bea told her about the six-month affair she had with a spiritual life coach and crystal enthusiast named Magic, who she met while perusing the gay self-help section of a Barnes and Noble. Which, Bea commented was strange, now that she was looking back on it, considering Magic had preached the importance of shopping small. So what had she been doing there in the first place? Bea had fallen deeply in love with Magic, came out of the closet for her, but two months after fleeing her abusive husband in the dead of night, came home to find Magic getting railed on both ends by butches wearing strap-ons—probably bought at a Spencer's. Cue the complete mental breakdown which led to her moving back in with her parents, who up until that point, she had been estranged from.

"Honestly," Gertie said, "that all seems pretty on par for messy coming out stories."

Bea blushed, her eyes softening. "You don't think I'm a mess?"

*I think you're a self-centered bitch the world would be better off without.* "Not at all. I get you wanting to take things slow." Gertie leaned close and rubbed Bea's shoulder.

"Well… And don't take this the wrong way, but Gertie, have you…"

"Have I…"

"Had sex with a woman before?"

Gertie shrugged. "No."

"Oh. No?" Bea shook her head. "That's—that's fine. It's just, um, queer sex can be a little more complicated. And Magic introduced me to some kinky stuff, so it's—my level is a little advanced."

"Your level? What is this, Tetris? What are you into? Kink? Like…spanking? Slapping? Leather?" *Is this bitch calling me vanilla to my face?* "Whatever you like, we can try it."

"The other thing—the other thing is that Magic was a top. Well, *usually*. She used a strap. And if you're not as experienced with sex, then…"

*Top, that reminds me. Maybe the gays don't own that word. Kink. Strap.* All of these words went far over Gertie's head, but she didn't want her confusion to show on her face. Wait, if Bea wanted her to top, that had to mean she was more submissive, right? *That* was a twist. Gertie assumed masculine-looking women would be tops; dominant, rough, ordering the other one about. *Very* interesting.

An image of Bea, sweaty and frothing at the mouth from being fucked too hard, surfaced in her mind. Abrupt, like a slap across the face. It was an image Gertie would masturbate to later that night, in the immaculate darkness of her bedroom, hoping her daughter wouldn't hear the lustful moans escaping her mouth.

Gertie knew she shouldn't want this, but to her shock—and elicit desire—she did.

"It's not a big deal. We can cross that bridge when we get to it." She squeezed Gertie's hands. "I want us to get to know each other. I don't want to get lost in lust. I really, really like you."

"I like you too."

"Really? Still?" Bea's eyes twinkled. "I don't even know how I got so lucky to meet you again."

Neither did Gertie.

# Chapter Six

"Have you tried pumping the accelerator as you turn the key?"

Gertie hovered outside in the driveway, phone in hand. She checked the time. 9:10 p.m. She didn't know what time June would get back, but she wanted to make sure Bea was out of here by then to avoid any awkward conversations. But her scrappy little Subaru would not budge. Bea turned the key over and over again, and the feral cat of an engine sputtered and spat in response. With a heavy sigh, Bea banged her head into the steering wheel.

"Do you want me to call someone?"

"Ugh…the battery might've died. I think I left the mirror light on or something."

"I can call someone," Gertie reiterated, resisting the urge to check her phone again. "Or I could just drive you home."

"And leave my car here?"

Gertie considered this. *Hmm.* She could probably find another use for the car, if Bea left it here for the night. Perhaps place a tracker in it, or rifle through the compartments for funsies. Not to mention, she could figure out where Bea lived for further observation if needed.

"Yeah, I can. Also, you drank a lot more than me. It'll be safer."

"Thank you," Bea whined, hopping out of the truck. "Sorry I'm such a mess."

They got in the truck and drove into the night, headlights peeling through the darkness of the surrounding forest. Bea provided her with directions that led back into town, past the shopping centers, to a quiet suburban area consisting of mostly ranch houses and ramblers with weeds so thick and dense that the individual leaves were clearly visible in the inky night. Streetlights with a strange, green hue flickered at random intervals. Bea shrunk lower and lower in her seat, but Gertie was so distracted by the shitty, pot-hole filled road that she couldn't even relish in her discomfort.

"This is the one."

They pulled into the driveway of a red ranch house with a ramshackle roof, whose shingles curled upward like the ends of a styled Barbie's hair. The garage door was wide open and underneath its orange light, warm like a furnace, two boys chased each other around a sedan. The smaller one, who was fair and blond, screeched with tears as he attempted to run away from the bigger boy, who held his fist high above his head. It was so small, almost not noticeable, but light bounced off something metal lodged between his knuckles.

"He's got a knife."

"What the fuck—*Trevor!*" Bea rolled down the window and shrieked with the fury of a banshee. "What the hell are you doing?"

Gertie put the car in park and climbed out as Bea did. She was curious. She had to see how this played out. River sprinted to his mother, sobbing, tears streaming from his gray eyes. Bea held up a reproachful finger to her other son, who laughed as he swaggered up to them, tracing the blade edge with a hungry desire.

"Where the hell did you get that?" Bea demanded. "And where are your grandparents?"

"I found it."

"Found it *where*, Trevor?"

The side door to the garage flew open, and a portly, mustachioed man exited the house. He was the wrinkliest person Gertie had ever seen—folds of skin stretched across his forehead, so heavy that they obscured his mean little eyes. With those flabby jowls, he was more bulldog than human.

"Nice of you to finally show up," Mr. Robinson said, snorting. "Did you forget I'm not a babysitter?"

"Dad," Bea cried out, "where did Trevor get a pocket-knife? Were you going to do anything?"

"Your kids are not my responsibility!"

"I was only gone for a few hours!"

River sniffled into his mother's shirt, but he looked up at Gertie with wide, curious eyes. Gertie couldn't help but stare at him. How did a child with a face this angelic come from one of the nastiest people she had ever known? After a few moments, Bea broke away from River and continued to shriek at her dad, who roared back at her with a fury that surprised even Gertie. Spittle flew from the man's face, and he shouted with such force that he wobbled on his own two stumpy feet. Definitely drunk, and definitely not a person to leave your children with.

River walked over to Gertie. "Hi."

"You okay?" She brushed back his bangs, inspecting for any wounds.

"He's fine. He's being a little faggot."

Gertie's eyes widened and she turned to look at the cunt—*teen*, she reminded herself—who was rolling the knife between his fingers, his expression unapologetic. Half-moons curved beneath his hollow eyes. Bea continued to shout and argue with her father in the background, and a woman who could only be her mother waddled out of the house to join the argument.

"Give me that," Gertie snapped, stretching out her hand.

"No," Trevor scoffed, giggling with the kind of mocking laughter that sent Gertie back to her high school days. Jack was always good to her, but his friends weren't. "Who the hell are you?"

"A friend of your mom's. You can call me Mrs. Burns."

"Nice to meet you, Mrs. Burns," River said hoarsely, rubbing his still-damp eyes.

"Not you. You can call me Gertie. *This* one can call me Mrs. Burns."

Trevor rolled his eyes.

Gertie snapped her fingers, demanding the knife again. "Give me the knife, or you'll be catching assault charges tonight."

"Fine. Fuck." He slapped it in her hand, a little too rough, tweaking her arm in the process. "Stupid bitch."

Gertie pocketed the knife but didn't budge from her spot.

"Are you the new dyke that's boning my mom?"

"Maybe I am. Meaning you had better act right, you little shit." Gertie smiled as Bea sauntered over to them, still red in the face from screaming at her father. River lifted a hand to his mouth to stifle his giggles. Trevor looked between the mothers, nostrils flared, and lips curled in a snarl. "Hey. Here it is."

Bea said her thanks before delivering a wallop to the back of Trevor's skull. "The next time I catch you terrorizing your brother, I'll do a lot worse than that. Do you understand me?"

"Now you discipline him!" Mr. Robinson snorted, tossing his head.

"Go in the house, Dad!" Bea screeched.

From across the street, a neighbor's porch light turned on—a warning sign to shut the fuck up before cops were called. Bea ushered her kids and parents inside the house before turning back to Gertie, eyes wide as the moon above them.

"I am—I am so sorry. This is not how I wanted this night to go."

"I know. It's okay." Gertie shoved her hands in her coat pockets. "I'll call you about your car tomorrow."

She hesitated, then kissed her cheek. Bea's eyes, tender with tears, softened into puddles. She hugged Gertie tight, and bid her goodnight. When Gertie was back in her car she jotted down the address, then took off. Trevor. What a little fuckwad. Such a nasty child. But River seemed sweet. She flinched, remembering that she had swept her hand across his forehead.

*Why did I do that?*

Once back at home, she finished the rest of the dishes, grabbed her laptop, and headed to bed to relax and do further research. After all, there was one more hurdle she had to face in building this facade: sex. If she wanted to really ruin Bea's life—to absolutely destroy her in every way possible—she had to give this woman the best sex of her life. The kind of sex where your body only responds to that other person's touch, where every line of their fingertips becomes imprinted on your skin and your soul, where you completely lose your sense of self. She didn't think it would be that hard to make a woman cum. After all, Jack had done it for her plenty of times, and that was without toys. How hard could it be?

She started off simple by visiting sites like *Autostraddle* before moving on to *Pornhub* and then *Ersties*. She googled—regrettably—some of the terms Bea had used. Strap was slang for strap-on. Good god, one of those things was *how much?* Why was gay sex so expensive? Or had prices changed that much in the five years since she'd bought her Hitachi wand?

She heard the front door click open. A notification popped up on her phone from her security camera. *"Mooom!"*

Gertie checked the time. 10:30 p.m. Damn, she was home early. She listened to the soft thumps of June's footsteps ascending the stairs, then she entered the room. Mascara confetti lined the undersides of her eyes, and all that remained of her lipstick was a mere collection of painted streaks on her face.

Gertie's stomach dropped. "What happened?"

"Nothing." June rubbed her eyes, still damp with tears. Then she crumpled, her voice splitting into sobs. Gertie held her arms open and June rushed over, collapsing into them. "Oh Mom, it's horrible. *Horrible.*"

"Why are you crying?"

"Reese. I asked Reese to dance with me, and he said no. He's dating Naya. *Naya.*" June sobbed louder, her distraught cries ripping from her throat.

Naya had been June's best friend since the third grade. Reese had been June's crush since sophomore year of school. Naya had broken girl code, and Reese had broken June's heart. *Got it.* Well, Naya had always been an attention-seeking little whore. When Gertie finally let June invite boys over for parties, Naya was always found alone with one in a closet, their pizza-greasy fingers jammed down the neckline of her shirt. It was only a matter of time before this happened.

"Oh sweetie, *what?*" Gertie cried out, feigning shock. "Naya knew you liked him!"

"I knoooowwwwww," June wailed. "I don't know what I'm gonna doooo! How am I going to face them on Monday?"

"Oh, Junebug, I'm so sorry. I don't have any answers for you honey, but is there something I can do to make you feel better? A bath, perhaps?"

June *loved* baths. She would take multi-hour long, bubbly soaks in her mother's jacuzzi until her skin was pruny from the water and her clay mask had dried to a crispy crust on her face. Since she was little, she struggled with panic attacks—the doctors never knew why, but Gertie figured out that baths helped her calm down pretty quick.

June agreed, and her lower lip wobbled before she

burst into tears again. Gertie gently brushed her aside to go turn on the water. She uncorked a fresh bottle of lavender bubble bath and poured it in, seething. June was too pretty to be jilted; far prettier than she had been at her age. And Reese wasn't too good-looking himself. As the years went by, men got worse, as evident from what she had seen with Trevor tonight.

*What is wrong with boys these days? What made them so callous and enraptured by the suffering of others?* God, if she ever saw that Reese again, she'd grab that boy by his stupid, square face, and smash it into a brick wall. She could picture the bristled texture grinding against his skin, the crooked branch of his nose splitting and the blood running into his mouth, choking him. Such a waste, such a—

—a gasp from June broke her reverie. She turned off the water and entered the bedroom again. Her laptop was wide open, and June was on it.

Looking at a big, black strap-on: 10 inches, veiny, and even more fun, it vibrated!

"June!"

The tears were gone from June's voice. "Why were you looking at this?"

Gertie snapped the lid shut. For a moment she wanted to scream at her, but she bit her tongue. *Stop. Be a good mom.* She clenched her jaw and waited for her daughter to speak, but she just stared at her. Slow realization spread across June's face and she clapped a hand over her mouth to hide her grin.

"Wait," June said. "Is this about your friend?"

Gertie didn't say anything.

June's jaw dropped and she scoffed with laughter. "Was this a date?"

Gertie held her breath and nodded. June squealed with ear-piercing joy, legs kicking in the air, the taffeta skirt of her magenta dress mushrooming upwards.

"Oh my god, *Mom!* You like her?"

Gertie was perplexed by June's emotions. She always was, but this time it was way too intense. Wouldn't it have been horrifying to discover your mother was queer? She'd been worried that if June found out, she would begin to question whether or not she had loved her father to begin with. Or worse, that if June found out, she would wonder why she hid it.

"This is so huge," June said, squeezing her mother's hands. "You don't date, at all, *ever*. You really like her? Honest?"

"I guess so," Gertie mumbled. "You don't think it's strange?"

"Everyone's gay now, Mom. Well, except for me. Unfortunately. Anyways," June chirped, "I'm really happy for you. When am I going to meet her?"

Gertie laughed, sheepish. "Well, we just started dating…"

"How long?"

"Tonight was our first date."

"Aww! Well I know it's like, really early, but I want to meet her! Is she a mom too? Do her kids go to Trinity Oaks?"

*Shit.*

Sweet little Junebug was as nosy as ever. There was no way Gertie could avoid them meeting now, despite her careful plans to avoid it.

This whole ordeal was about to get a helluva lot messier.

# Chapter Seven

Four weeks and five family dinners later, Bea and June became friends. Much to Gertie's disgust. She'd watch them at the dinner table, talking and laughing and sharing stories and if Gertie had to listen to their trilling "OMGs" and "Seriouslys" and "For reals" and "Oh my *GODs*" and "No ways", she was going to be sick.

Gertie hoped that when she invited Bea for a family meal, she would say it was too soon to meet June. However, Bea was all too eager. As it turned out, Bea had taken up cheering in high school to pass as straight—*Go Grizzlies, woo!*—so she had that in common with June. Gertie refrained from rolling her eyes when they practiced handstands and cartwheels in the garden after dinner, but she did feel a slight curl in her lips when June smiled. By the third meeting, they even greeted each other with a coordinated cheer. What a monstrous feeling, to know that your one and only daughter was kinning with your worst enemy.

But Bea did take June's mind off Reese, so at least there was an upside.

It didn't take too long before the town got hold of the fact that Gertie Burns, widow-turned-saint extraordinaire, was now dating again. At the last PTA meeting before the Parents' Night event, she found herself answering deeply personal questions for the other biddies, who were curious as to why she had "gone gay". God, they were more interested in this debacle than they were with her having announced her candidacy.

"Well," Misty said, "you need to bring her to the event. We're all curious about this mystery woman." The way she said "woman", with that unpleasant tang hiding on her tongue.

*Bitch.*

"Yeah," Kellyanne added, glancing up from her phone. "How come I can't find her on Facebook?"

"She's not a huge social media person."

"Is she even real?" Misty held up a hand to block her gap-toothed smile.

Gertie's posture stiffened as a hush fell over the group.

Misty looked between the shocked members, suppressing a nervous laugh. "I mean, I didn't think you'd ever date. You seemed so turned off to the idea. Remember the time I set you up with that widower?"

"Which one?" Joanna asked.

"Ted Gustafo."

"Ohhh, Ted. I like Ted. Nice guy."

"I did too. But this one…" Misty swiveled her head back around to face Gertie. "This one went out with him and barely spoke the whole time."

"What?" Kellyanne asked, her jaw all but dropping to the floor.

"That's not true."

But it was. Misty had nagged and nagged her to give this guy a chance, and when she finally caved and went on the date, she brought along a book and read through most of the meal. His self-esteem was low enough to let her do that.

*Pathetic.*

"Don't take this the wrong way, Gert, but sometimes you seem aloof. It's not a good look to voters." Misty pushed back some of her cuticles in an effort to avoid eye contact. "I think dating someone could help you with this creepy-widow imagery you've got going on."

"Wait a minute. A creepy widow? Who thinks I'm a creepy widow?"

The room was silent. Gertie swallowed her anger, a lump of thumbtacks that pricked her throat on the way down.

"You're *sure* I look okay?" Bea whined, adjusting her bowtie in the mirror again. "I can dress more femme if you'd like."

"No," Gertie protested, clasping the back of her earring. "You're perfect."

Gertie was wearing an autumn-yellow tea dress with a sweetheart neckline, while Bea wore a fitted suit in a matching shade. Standing side-by-side in the mirror, they resembled a sapphic sun, glittering and prideful.

"Besides, I don't know why *you're* fussing when *I* look like a frog."

"Hey!" Bea snapped, snatching her wrist and pulling her close. "You look ravishing, alright? These skinny bitches *wish* they could wear a dress that makes their ass and tits look this good. And your makeup is flawless. You look *hot*."

Gertie couldn't help but blush. Bea was crude, but damn if she wasn't honest. Gertie turned to the side in her mirror and admired the sensuous curves of her body. Since she started seeing Bea, she was seeing her body in a whole new light. Whenever they met, Bea had something to compliment her on, even if it was mundane. Perhaps there was a benefit to keeping her around—

—well, longer than originally intended.

She still had to do the revenge thing.

Gertie checked her teeth in the mirror. The auburn lipstick stains looked like dried blood. With the tip of her tongue, she licked them away.

Laughing. They were all laughing at Bea, but in a good way. Gathered underneath the chandelier in the Trinity Oaks ballroom, Gertie watched with amazement as Bea entertained her stuck-up friends with a rousing tale of when she figured out her old dog had eaten an entire spool of thread. Spoiler alert: when it came out his ass.

Misty wiped a stray tear from her eyes and patted Gertie's shoulder, weighing it down with the heavy golden bangles that clattered around her bird-thin wrist. She'd only drank a single glass of champagne, but she was already bubbly from the bubbly. Probably "pregamed" before she got there.

"I am *so* glad you're not hiding her from us anymore," Misty said, a slight slur to the words. "God, she is a delight."

"I don't think she was *hiding* me, per se," Bea said, winking at Gertie as she slipped an arm around her waist. "She's a busy woman."

"Right. How's the campaign going?"

"Ordered the posters the other day. When those come in, this one will be helping me put them up around town." She might as well make Bea do some menial labor for her. "And I've hired someone to build a website."

Joanna wrinkled her nose. "A website? Seems extra."

"Well, I want to set myself above the competition."

"Good that you hired help." Misty took another sip. "My dear, I love you, but you cannot design anything to save your life."

Gertie smiled, her fingers grasping onto the champagne flute a little too tight. She took a sip and set it down on one of the banquet tables, contributing to the existing graveyard of them. Before Gertie could comprehend what was happening, Bea excused them from the conversation and whisked her out to the dance floor, where an upbeat pop song was beginning to play.

"Figured I should rescue you," Bea said with a smile, placing her hands on Gertie's waist. "Misty's got a lot of shit to say, huh?"

"When doesn't she?" Gertie rolled her eyes, and then realized they were at a complete standstill, Bea's hands on her body with a decided firmness akin to a potter spinning ceramics. Apprehensive, she placed her hands on Bea's shoulders.

"I promise I won't step on your toes."

"It's not that..." Gertie trailed off, unsure of how to tell this woman that she abhorred being touched by her. *But then again, do I?*

They were almost cheek to cheek now. Bea smelled so pleasant tonight. She wore a cedar cologne that was less offensive to her senses than these men who reeked of scotch. She wasn't offended by standing this close to her. Didn't feel the same urge to bleach her flesh as she had weeks ago when this first started. Hell, she felt...comfortable.

When was the last time she danced like this? Obviously, when Jack was alive, but she couldn't remember exactly. She remembered they'd been preparing dinner in the kitchen, baby June snacking on Cheerios in her highchair. She remembered she had been whisking a bowl of something; had kept it miraculously tucked under her arm as he had spun her across the linoleum floor. And she remembered the firmness of his hands against her lower back, the same firmness she felt from Bea now, making her feel so safe, and not at all small.

"You're getting the hang of it," Bea said.

"You know something?" Gertie's voice was thin, but she didn't know why. "This is the song that Jack and I...this was the first song we danced to at our wedding."

For a moment, she felt self-conscious. Would she live the rest of her life bringing up Jack, and comparing everything to him? Would Bea become frustrated and dump her before she had a chance to enact her revenge?

But Bea smiled. "It's a nice first dance song."

"Y-yeah."

"Better than a ballad version of *Centerfold*."

"Yours?"

Bea nodded, rolling her eyes. Gertie laughed, resting her forehead against Bea's shoulder.

"Do you want to keep dancing? If this is a song meant

for you and Jack, I don't want to overstep."

"No, no. This is fine. He would be mad at me if I didn't dance."

That was the truth. Jack got frustrated when she sat by the sidelines too long. He was always the one encouraging her to try new things. Bea was the same way. Come to think of it, this was the second time they'd done something that reminded her of Jack. Danced to this song, and then the daisies. Those five daisies in that little bouquet from their first date.

Maybe this was Jack's handiwork. Maybe he'd reached from beyond the veil to assure her that she had his blessing. But Jack didn't know this wasn't real. The very thought made Gertie want to cry. He had always seen the best parts of her; had no idea how deep the darkness lurked beneath. If this was his way of telling her that he wanted her to move on, then she was forsaking him by playing this game of revenge.

When the song ended, Gertie broke away from Bea, stumbling through a whispered apology. She headed into the hallway, away from the flashing lights and throngs of people, hoping to find solace, but Bea followed her.

"Gertrude." Her hand squeezed hers. "Talk to me."

"I can't," Gertie sniffled, using her fingers to carefully dab away her tears. "I don't know what came over me."

"You're grieving. It's okay."

"It's been too long for it to feel this raw." Anger bit into her voice, but it only made her weep harder.

Bea shook her head. "Grief isn't linear. It's cyclical."

"What?"

"It comes back. Like the ocean tides," Bea said, tucking a strand of her curly black hair behind her ear. "Sometimes it's going to fill up every part of you."

"I'm embarrassed."

"Don't be." Bea smiled. "If you're sad, you can cry it out. It's okay."

So Gertie continued to weep, until after a few minutes, she collected herself, and danced with Bea again. When the party ended, she drove Bea home—her car was still on the fritz—and after pulling into the driveway, they sat in the car for several minutes. Sweat clung to the undersides of Gertie's breasts and between the silken folds of her body, and the mid-autumn heat did little to alleviate her discomfort.

"It was great meeting your friends. Although…you're sure you're okay with us moving this fast?"

"I don't think it's moving too fast if it feels this right."

Gertie resisted the urge to pump her fist in triumph when she saw the melted smile spread across Bea's face, so infatuated. They leaned in to kiss again, Bea's hands soft against her round cheeks, and Gertie felt this strange flutter in her chest. Something about this night had changed her, had changed them. It was frustrating, terrifying, exciting—a cliff diver at the precipice of jumping. But just as she began to enjoy it, they were interrupted by the sharp knock of Mr.

Robinson's fist against the window. Startled, the two pulled away from each other, Bea yelping in surprise. Gertie cracked the window.

"Don't loiter in my driveway," Mr. Robinson snarled at Gertie. He looked past her at his daughter. "Get in my house."

"What is his problem?" Gertie muttered, glancing over at Bea. "Did he not know you were going out tonight?"

"Oh he knew. He didn't want me to. If he had it his way, he'd lock me up in a room and never let me out."

Another sharp clash of knuckles against glass. "Now, Beatrice."

Like a petulant teenager, Bea threw open the door with a huff and stomped into the house. Gertie sat in the driver's seat, watching Mr. Robinson hover outside her window. He scraped his boots against the crackled asphalt like he was trying to wipe off dog shit, and snorted phlegm before spewing it onto the ground.

"Ever since my daughter started seeing you, she's been talking back more. I don't like it, and I don't like you."

"You do know that your daughter is a grown woman, right?"

"Doesn't mean she knows what's best for herself. It's wrong for her to bring you around her damn kids. They don't need to see this shit."

"Well, they didn't." She stared at the little man's angry

face, so gnarled and twisted like a tree trunk. Goddamn, that's the face of a man who should've been dead decades ago. "I know you're concerned about your daughter and your grandsons, and I can assure you I only have serious intentions. I'm not like the other woman she's dated."

"I know," he snapped. "You're worse. Least the last one was pretty. You look like Humpty Dumpty and have an ass like him, too."

Gertie smiled wide, her voice an echo of politeness. "Unfortunately, it's not about what *you* like in a woman. After all, I'm not dating you. I would be loath to."

"That's the problem with you dykes. You're all so fucking twisted that you'll never know the love of a good man." He spat another wad of mucus onto the driveway, narrowly missing her car. "Bea wasn't like that until women like you showed up."

"Bea wasn't like that because you allowed her to be abused. By both her husband and your brother."

He stared at her, his gaze hard. Gertie pursed her lips together, trying to suppress the knowing smile itching to spread across her face.

"Her Uncle Earnest was *your* brother, right?"

The folds of his forehead lifted, revealing the whites of his surprised eyes. He shuffled back from the car, as if worried he would be struck. He was right to worry. Gertie felt like swinging.

"Mmmhmm. Right. I'm curious."

"About what?"

"Why you did it. Why you helped your brother."

"I didn't—"

Gertie laughed with the vivacity of Maleficent, haughty and triumphant and oh-so-done with his shit. Then her mask dropped. Fish-like eyes stared back at him with contempt, one corner of her mouth curled back in a disgusted grimace.

"Where there's a paper trail, there's a way, Donald Michael Robinson."

Oh, that spooked him. "D-Don't come 'round here again. If you do, we're gonna have a problem."

"Oooh," Gertie said, clicking her tongue against her teeth. She flipped the truck into reverse and inched out of the driveway. "I'm almost scared. Maybe if you stapled some of that skin above your eyes, I could see your nasty expression better. If you want, someday I can arrange that for you."

Someday very, *very* soon. Sooner than he would think. Driving home that night, Gertie stewed in her homicidal thoughts. *Fuck Donald. Fuck that pedophile sympathizing bastard, and fuck his wife Lynda too.*

He was more annoying than he was a threat, but Gertie didn't like the fact that he talked to her with such homophobic repulsion. Plus, if he was going to interrupt her plans with Bea, then he needed to go. Like it or not, tonight had revealed that Gertie *needed* Bea. At least for a little while longer, maybe until she won the election. Her charm, charisma, and good humor could make her look less like a "creepy widow" in the eyes of the voters.

At the same time, she still needed to ruin Bea's life. What better way to do that than by snipping holes in her safety net? By taking out her parents, Bea would have nowhere to live. She'd be financially destitute. That seemed like a worthwhile first move in her revenge plan. Still, with the election on the line, she was hesitant to get her hands dirty.

The good thing about bucket loads of money was, she wouldn't have to.

# Chapter Eight

Earl Rose was the kind of man you'd least expect to be a fixer, aside from the fact that his hands were always dirty. An avid gardener, Earl spent every Saturday and Sunday tending to his vegetable garden, plentiful with carrots, potatoes, and cabbages. Dirt was, in fact, so much a part of him that it filled the creases on his knuckles and knees like a permanent, unfashionable tattoo. Aside from this, he had a clean appearance. Bushy Santa beard, immaculately-shaped eyebrows, and a round jawline like the underside of an egg. Gertie had been referred to him through her P.I., who had referred her to another P.I., who referred her to his cousin, who "knew a guy". After exchanging a series of emails—she had been told to ask him to "trim the roses"—he agreed to meet at her house the following Saturday morning, when June was at cheer practice.

"So two people?" he asked her. "How old?"

"Sixties, maybe seventies?" She winced, knowing he

was not much younger than they were.

He nodded. "That'll be easy."

"Really?"

"All we have to do is figure out when they're going somewhere, and I'll cut the brake lines to their car. Piece of cake. These people like to travel? Heading for the highway anytime soon?"

"It has to be a highway?"

"They have to be going fast enough to die if they crash. If they're just going down the street to the grocery store, they'll get clipped—*at best*—and end up with some property damage. But you want them dead-dead, so again, any highway travel planned?"

Gertie shook her head.

Earl stroked his beard, leaning back on the sofa. It crinkled and squeaked beneath him, and he frowned, uncomfortable. "Well, that's what you'll have to figure out then."

"And what do I do?"

He shrugged. "Just call me. I'll be around."

"For payment…"

"You're going to make a check in the amount of $250,000 to Rose Landscaping Services LLC. And if anyone asks you about it, it's to service the garden you have here." He turned to look out the back window, an appreciative smile on his face. "You're the first client I've worked with where that would actually be a feasible excuse for dropping that chunk of change. The rest I've had to build gardens for."

"Gardens?"

"Landscaping is my primary business. Fixing is my second." He withdrew a business card from his wallet and offered it to her. Small roses and vines curled around the elegant black letters. "And hey, if I get the layout of your garden, well, it makes it easier to plant bodies if needed."

"I can't have bodies being buried here."

"Oh, it's just a hypothetical." He waved a dismissive hand. "Anyways, I'll expect the check before I expect the call, Gertie."

"Really?" She was baffled as he rose to his feet with a grunt. *Wouldn't the payout happen after the hit?*

"Yes, really. You pay me upfront to do the job, and keep me quiet." He tapped his forehead a few times, then pressed his finger to his lips. He smiled. "I'll see myself out."

So Gertie waited for an opportunity, her patience wilting like vines in the winter. She put up with Donald's insulting barrage whenever she dropped Bea at home, and spent her days with the PTA or building her campaign. After work, Bea would join her for canvassing, and the two would patrol the neighborhoods to drop off fliers together and schmooze constituents. When Gertie couldn't charm them—rugged blue-collar men, exhausted housewives who needed a good laugh, highly personable gays—Bea would do it for her.

Little by little, Bea was proving her usefulness, and

though she was irritated, Gertie was even being swayed by the power of her smile. They opened up to each other more and more. Gertie found herself telling stories about Jack, and Bea talked about the trauma she had experienced at the hands of her uncle and ex-husband, sometimes describing it with disturbing detail. Sometimes after exchanging stories, they would be moved to the point of tears. Gertie had laughed with Jack many times, and she had been at home with him in those moments. But until she had started dating Bea, she never realized the comfort of sitting in your sadness while someone held your hand. Jack wanted to fix, but Bea welcomed emotional turmoil like an old friend.

All the while, she kept an open ear, listening for any possibilities of slaughtering the Robinsons. Her chance came after Trevor had, in another of his rageful outbursts, burned down the rose bushes that his grandparents had lovingly tended to for the 26 years they'd owned the home. To replace the bushes, they would have to go to the Gerten's Gardens off the highway exit, a good twenty-minute drive from town.

*Trevor, you magnificent fuckwad.*

After wiring her payment, Gertie called Earl and he snuck into the garage that night to tamper with the brakes. The next afternoon, she found herself hunched in the passenger seat of his Mustang, an oversized pair of sunglasses eclipsing her face. She'd insisted she had to see this to the end, something that had pissed off Earl to no end, but he gave in when she offered an extra 5K to sweeten the deal. They tailed the Robinsons' car far enough so that they were just a blip on the horizon. Gertie had to stare at them through a pair of binoculars to keep track of where they were going.

"I don't understand," she said. "Shouldn't they be spinning out?"

"When you tamper with the brakes, you can't break through them completely," Earl told her. "Otherwise they would have broken them in town, and again—"

"Yeah, yeah, we need speed."

"It's a nice day," he told her. "Overcast. Not too busy."

"So?"

"Look around." He waved a finger in a circle. "Not a lot of cars coming and going."

Gertie lifted the binoculars again. The trembling dot of their car swerved from side to side. Tingling with excitement, Gertie squeezed Earl's arm, urging him to speed up. The dot became bigger and bigger the closer they approached, and they watched the car careen off the road, right through the guardrail, into the thorny thicket. Earl pulled off to the shoulder, and Gertie pressed her face against the window, a child in a candy store eager to see the gooiest pieces of fudge.

In this case, the gooey pieces of fudge would've been their bloated, bloody bodies.

At the foot of the hill, just visible from the roadway, rested the smoldering car, its front end impaled by the trunk of a tree. Glass littered the ground like confetti. Oil pooled underneath the mechanical catastrophe, charcoal-black smoke escaped its pores in wisps and puffs.

"There you go," Earl grumbled.

Gertie shook her head. She unbuckled her seatbelt and exited the car, ignoring Earl's cries of protest. She skidded down the treacherous hillside, sloppy with mud from where the car had left tracks. The slope was so steep that her sunglasses slipped down to the very tip of her nose. Earl scrambled after her, grumbling and cursing beneath his breath.

Tiptoeing over the car's crushed organs, she approached the driver's side window, her heartbeat quickening with excitement. The tree trunk had smashed through the dashboard, stray strips of jagged bark and branches jutting through the deflating airbags. The Robinsons lay in their seats, heads thrown back, jaws slack, blood dripping from noses and open mouths. Gertie glanced down and saw that the front end of the car and steering wheel had crushed the front of Donald's knees, almost severing them. Bleached bone poked through gaping, gushing wounds in the right leg, the sinews of muscle splintering away from the mess as if trying to escape. The left leg was worse—that knee was a bowl of blended beet soup. One of his hands was pinned beneath the steering wheel, a few fingers smashed against the palm like the spring of a jack-in-the-box poised for launch. Wrinkles and folds of fat and bone spread out, dripping to the simmering car floor.

Despite this carnage, she noticed one tragic thing.

They were both still breathing. Shallow, but distinctive from the way that their chests heaved. Like newborn babes, their bleary eyes searched for solace, their mouths opened to moan in an intonation similar to that of lambs led to slaughter.

"They're not dead," she snapped at Earl.

"They'll be dead before anyone finds them. I can promise you that."

"No." Gertie shook her head. "They *have* to be dead. I told you that. I can't take any risks. Besides, if they're not dead, then Bea will be roped into taking care of their sorry asses."

Earl rolled his eyes and shrugged.

Gertie crossed her arms. "Tell me what I have to do to make this happen."

"If you do *anything* to them, your fingerprints will be on the scene."

"So we have to burn the car, is what you're saying? Leave no trace of evidence?"

"The car will light on fire if we leave it long enough."

"Hey!" Gertie snapped, her voice ferocious. "I paid you *good* money to make sure these bastards were dead, and that didn't happen. We aren't leaving until this fucking prick has his windpipe crushed in."

She could hear the throaty, wordless rasping of Donald

in the front seat. She glanced back and saw that he'd turned his head to face her, his eyes slowly widening and retracting, trying to focus. He recognized her. And from the way his brows furrowed, he knew she was responsible.

Gertie rolled her eyes. "Oh please. Don't tell me you're surprised by this."

Flustered but irritated, Gertie scoured the ground for something she could use. She found a twisted piece of metal, likely some broken piece from the hood. It was sharp and shaped like an icicle, perfect for poking more holes in that bastard. Gertie leaned through the driver's side window, face to face with Donald, whose rancid breath invaded her nostrils and made her stomach gurgle. He opened his mouth to speak, but all that came out were teeth and some flabby bits of gum tissue. She pressed the tip of the metal shard against his neck, and he coughed, droplets of blood spattering her face. She didn't flinch.

"Feels sharp, doesn't it?" she whispered. "Sharp. Like someone forcing themselves inside your body. Can you imagine that kind of pain at ten years old?"

His eyes, mere pinpricks in a sea of white, focused on the weapon that was pressed against his flesh.

"Huh? Can you?" she chuckled, giddy, blood rushing to her head. "You know, she also couldn't speak, because your brother had shoved his sock down her throat. But it wouldn't have mattered anyway, because when this was all happening, what did you do, Donald? What did you do?"

Wet tears dripped down to mingle with droplets of sweat surfacing on his face.

"You turned up the volume on the TV," Gertie hissed through gritted teeth. "And pretended not to hear her."

He whimpered, completely at her mercy, and unable to fight back.

God, this had been *so* worth the money.

Gertie pushed the tip of the shard through his flesh, slow and meticulous. A few droplets spurted out like food from a bratty toddler's mouth—phlegmy and thick—splashing against the steering wheel. He wriggled from side to side in an attempt to escape, which only made the shredded hole in his neck grow bigger. She could feel the resistance of muscles, could see the pool of blood trying to fill the gory space. Donald's eyes rolled upward as his body began to spasm, and his chest shuddered in rolls of thunder. She could've stopped with one hole in his throat, that was for sure.

But she was going to let this fucker really have a taste of what it meant to feel helpless. If Gertie was the lion and they were the gazelles, then this metal shard would be her teeth and claws. And she was all too eager to tear them apart.

She ripped the shard from the hole, and he wheezed blood, thrashing in place. She drove it into his shoulder, and carved a curve down the center of his chest—a perfect impression of a waxing moon. Ribbons of blood coursed down his body onto the floor. She could hear Linda cry, even protest, but he still couldn't speak. Giggling, Gertie stabbed him again in the thigh, ripping open the artery, which erupted like Mt. Vesuvius.

*One more thing.*

She plunged through the center of his trembling eye, which had always regarded her with such disgust. She penetrated deep into the cavern of his skull and battered around his scrambled brains, writhing in pleasure as she did so. *Fuck, this is better than sex.*

It was only then that Linda screamed through a gargle of her own blood. Gertie leaned out the driver's side window and raced around the side, ignoring a perturbed Earl, who reached into his back pocket for a matchbook. This time, Gertie didn't savor it as much. She stabbed Linda over and over in her throat, each strike tenderizing the meat that connected her head to the rest of her body until she was all but decapitated.

Earl spat on the ground in frustration. "Jesus, Gertie. What a mess you've made."

Panting, Gertie's trembling hands scratched at her jeans, trying to remove the blood and grime lodged beneath her nails. Earl struck a match and added it to the smoldering fire brewing under the hood. A pop here, a poof there, and within seconds, it was engulfed in flames. Earl prodded her at the small of her back, encouraging her to leave. They scrambled up the hill, then took off before the flames rose over the treetops.

"It would've worked, you psycho," Earl yelled, smacking his open palm against the top of his steering wheel. "Did you have to go and do that?"

Gertie reached into her purse—sitting on the dash—and withdrew a few trusty wet wipes to clean off her bloodstained hands. She never knew how dark some of the tissues in the human body could be. Some were as black and clotted as uterine lining; others pink and soft like chewed-up bubblegum. She felt guilty as she cleaned herself, like she was destroying a work of art.

"They were child molester sympathizers, so yes, I actually had to do that."

"I thought you didn't care about this damn woman you were with."

Gertie hesitated, then whispered, "I don't."

# Chapter Nine

Six hours passed before Bea got the call about the car accident. Luckily, the fire burned most of their bodies, and the officer at the scene told her the coroner didn't have much to recover. Gertie praised herself for this—not only had she gotten to kill those fuckers, her on-scene cremation was a success, too. Unfortunately, Bea wouldn't know to appreciate her for this cost-saving measure, but she *did* appreciate Gertie for comforting her. The night that her parents passed, the trauma of her childhood resurfaced in the ugliness of her grief. Bea drove herself and the boys over to the house, then crawled into bed with her. For some odd reason, Gertie couldn't delight in Bea's misery. She could only stroke her head over and over again, sympathetic tears pricking at the corners of her eyes, arms shaking as she cradled a woman who mourned the protectors she never had.

In the early morning when Gertie came to, she found

Bea lying wide awake, staring at the ceiling with a catatonic expression. Gertie yawned a good morning, but Bea didn't say it back, and the rejection stung a little. They lay there for a while in the dusky darkness of her bedroom, golden ribbons of sunlight streaming through gaps in the black-out curtains.

"I have nowhere to live." Bea broke the silence. "I can't live in that house. Even if I could afford it, I won't."

"I'm sorry." For once, Gertie felt like she meant it, and grimaced to herself.

"Not your fault."

Gertie winced. Bea didn't notice.

"I guess that's it then. Me and the boys are going to live out of my car." Her voice broke, and she buried her face in her hands once more, sobbing. "God, it's like as soon as my life gets better, it all comes crashing down. I don't—I don't know what I'm doing wrong. I feel like I'm cursed." In a way, she was. But Gertie insisted that she wasn't, enveloping Bea in her arms and allowing her to cry some more.

"I…I'm so sorry. I don't know what this means for us," Bea gasped through her sobs, snot bubbling in her nostrils. "I don't know w-what I'm going to do, Gertie. God help me."

"God won't help you." Gertie brushed the tears from her face with her thumb. "I will."

At that moment, Gertie felt like her soul had fled her body. *What?* That declaration felt instinctual. An out of body experience. She had to look at her hands to figure out if she was really herself or not. Damn. She was. Bea's eyes widened with realization, her jaw dropping.

"What—what do you mean by that?" Bea asked. "You'd let me live with you?"

"I mean...I was going to ask you anyways," Gertie replied. "I knew you had to leave your parents' soon, especially if we ever wanted any modicum of privacy. And also because they were terrible to you."

"You don't think it's too soon?"

"If anything, not soon enough. We're not getting any younger. What are we waiting for?"

"Oh my God." Bea's voice shifted to a lighter tone, and although she sobbed, it was from relief, not from pain, and Gertie saw her shoulders loosen a little. Bea kissed Gertie's cheeks multiple times, squeezing her tight. "I love you. I love you, Gertrude. Have I ever told you that?"

She had. Multiple times. Mostly under her breath, when they bid each other goodnight after a date, as if to practice it. She didn't think Gertie could hear her back then. But Gertie could hear her now, loud and clear. For some reason, her body was flooded with feelings of nervousness rather than disgust. She kissed Bea back, allowing the woman to press her down against the pillows. Damn. Perhaps her game of revenge had evolved somewhat. Gertie was flexible. It wasn't the first time her life plans had encountered a drastic change.

At least this time, it hadn't resulted in tragedy. In fact,

it felt rather good. Bea, eager to please, pressed kisses against her neck and collarbone. Unbuttoned the top of her night-gown and massaged her breasts in slow, circular motions. This was the furthest they were able to go since that first dinner date, as they never had privacy. Gertie returned Bea's kisses in earnest, touching her in kind, the two of them stripping off their pajamas. Bea sucked on two of her fingers, pulling them out with a wet *pop!* before using them to circle Gertie's clit. Her gaze was intense, fascinated by the way Gertie's vagina slurped on her digits. It felt good, the way they rubbed and explored each ridge, delicately mapping out the area as if to commit it to memory.

"I thought you didn't want to top?" Gertie asked, biting down on her lip to suppress her moans. Her breath shuddered in her chest.

"Oh, I don't," Bea grinned. "But I want to make sure you get off first."

Bea bent her head low, mouth open, and Gertie couldn't help but lift her hips to meet her. Bea's eyes closed, and her tongue became a paintbrush that covered the canvas in long, bold strokes. Each arm wrapped around Gertie's thighs, and she lifted them, bringing her legs over her shoulders. Gertie gasped, feeling more exposed. She groaned when Bea's tongue entered her body, her hands grasping her breasts with a surprising possessiveness. Bea slurped and moaned, not stopping to even take a breath. It didn't take long before Gertie came, her choked cries escaping, her body ignited.

Triumphant, Bea pulled away and wiped her mouth with the back of her hand. She beamed from ear to ear. Gertie blushed, embarrassed by the damp streaks across Bea's mouth. But Bea stroked the insides of her thighs reassuringly, her gaze lustful, her body hungering for more.

"I could go for round two, if you'd like. Or...you could do something to me, instead."

Gertie sat on her knees, exchanging kisses with Bea before pushing her down against the mattress. "You know, you never told me what you were into."

Bea giggled. "What?"

"You said you were kinky but you never specified." Gertie smiled teasingly, tracing the nape of her neck. The woman quivered at her touch. "I've been studying up."

"You're sure you want to try them? There's a lot."

"Can you get off without them?"

She giggled again, shaking her head.

"Well, let's hear it."

"Okay. Um...I like bondage. I don't like being tied to the bed, but I like being tied up by my wrists. Love being dominated."

Gertie had expected as such. "So, when you're domi-nated, do you...want to be treated rough?"

A blush darkened Bea's cheeks. "I love being hit, spanked, insulted. And I like—I like being choked. Also a little bit of non-con. You know what that is?"

Gertie nodded. All of this was relatively tame, per her research. "Do you use any safe words?"

"Safe words feel weird to me, actually. I'm good with just—no, or stop, or..." Bea gave a nervous laugh, a strange emotion surfacing in her eyes. "For me...I like the idea of being—of being hurt by someone I can trust. Someone who will stop when I tell them to."

The admission felt like a gut punch to Gertie. *Ahh.* So this is why she was into kink. A safe way for her to explore the trauma she'd been subjected to. A way to reclaim that violence for herself. A wave of sadness crashed over her, stifling the smile on her face.

Bea averted her eyes. "I know, I know, I'm pretty bent."

"Don't feel ashamed." Gertie squeezed her hands. "This is all fine with me. Not weird at all."

"Really?"

Gertie nodded, her smile firm. "Really. I'm not scared."

"Well, I'm glad...*Oh!* Oh. There's also one...*big, big* thing—and I don't expect you to try this—but...knife play."

"Knife play?"

"I like having a knife held up to my throat while someone is on top of me."

*What the fuck?* This wasn't on the kink forums. Was this a part of non-con or was this something completely different?

"Would I cut you?" Gertie asked, confused.

"No!" Bea laughed. "No, no cutting or slicing. Some people like that, but I don't go that far. Too much clean up."

"So no cutting, it's just kinda…there."

"Yep! And look—I don't expect you to want to try that. Even if we did, we could use a prop knife. It doesn't have to be real."

"But do you *like* the real knife?"

"I do. I kinda like the threat to be real."

The same image of Bea writhing beneath her in reckless abandon now had a new detail to it. She pictured Bea's tongue licking the edge of the blade with caution, begging her to go in deeper.

*Oh no.*

"You want to try it?" Bea must've been able to tell how red her face was. "You sure?"

Gertie nodded. Retreating from the bedroom, she tiptoed downstairs to the kitchen, and grabbed a small steak knife, something that would give her easy control. She went back upstairs, retrieved her strap-on from the chest in her walk-in closet, and slipped it on. Bea waited for her in bed, naked, draped across the sheets like a subject posing for a painting. With her swollen lips and voluptuous breasts, she might as well have been one.

Gertie crawled on top of her, nudging her legs apart. She withdrew a bottle of lube from the nightstand, and poured it over her silicone dick. She teased Bea's body, pinching and licking her nipples, stroking her throbbing clit. Bea moaned and thrust back against her fingers, whispered cuss words between gasps of pleasure. Once she was sufficiently prepared, she hooked her hands underneath her knees and pried her legs apart. Bea moaned as she felt the dick push deep inside her, her chest shuddering with excitement. Gertie pushed in, careful and slow. She wanted to be delicate, to savor the moment.

And she didn't know why.

Bea instructed her on how to move her hips, and Gertie soon got the hang of it, adopting a rolling motion that pushed into the deepest parts of Bea's body before quickly receding. Once she figured that out, she lifted the steak knife, and held it close to Bea's throat. Bea squealed in pleasure when Gertie thrust into her harder, the steak knife hovering in place at her carotid artery. She could feel Bea's body tighten around her, watched as the woman's hands gripped the sheets and her face contorted in a mixture of pleasure and pain. Gertie trailed the tip of the knife from her chin to the center of her breasts, to the area right above her pubic bone.

"Tell me how you want me to split you open," Gertie growled. "I could do it with my cock, or this knife. Your call."

And Bea responded in kind.

Breathless, the two laid in a tangled heap of sheets, the stench of sex and sweat tangible in the air. The knife abandoned long ago to the floor, having been replaced by Gertie's hand, wrapped tight around Bea's skin. Only for a few moments until she'd made that incredible, lustful, orgasm face.

Bea snuggled against Gertie, one leg looped over hers, her skin flushed. Residual trembles coursed through her body, a souvenir of a fantastic sexual escapade. She planted kisses on Gertie's neck and chest with the reverence of someone worshipping an altar.

"That was perfect," Bea whispered.

"Was it?"

"I came like, three times," she giggled. "And here I expected you wouldn't be that good of a top the first time around. You're full of surprises."

"I *did* study up. I told you that."

"I know. But reading about it and watching it is different from the real thing." Bea's fingers traced the insides of Gertie's thighs. "Did you like it?"

"I loved it."

To her horror—and pleasant surprise—she had. To be in a position of power was something she got more pleasure from than the sex itself. And the imagery…the facial expressions, the way her breasts swelled with pleasure, the visible trembles of her thighs, these were things Gertie committed to memory.

*Huh.* She was *actually* queer after all.

"You know what, you didn't say it back."

"What?"

"I said I loved you. You didn't say it back," Bea chuckled. "It's fine. I don't need you to say it out loud. I think I know your feelings."

"You do?"

"You seem like the type that loves fast and hard." Bea said, a mischievous smirk teasing at the corner of her lips. "No? Wishful thinking?"

Wishful thinking would be an understatement. Gertie had only ever loved Jack with an unshakable certainty. She didn't even know if she loved June. She wasn't swept with emotion when she gazed at her face the way she did with Jack. She had a motherly instinct to protect her and help her succeed, but she didn't know if she would call that love so much as a biological override. She supposed she loved June in the way her father had loved her, just with a little more warmth. June knew she could go to her for anything and trust her mother to keep her secrets—and so far in her life, June had never done anything bad enough to warrant Gertie exploiting said secrets.

At times Gertie did feel guilty. Were it not for her postpartum depression and Jack's death, she wondered if her heart would have developed properly. That she would've been able to feel an intense and fierce love for June, as all the parenting books had told her she would. If her mother was here,

103

she would've asked her questions, but every time she thought of her, it felt like tearing a scab off an old wound. It didn't succeed in doing anything except making her bleed.

She had decided long ago that it was best to accept her feelings for what they were, rather than question *why* they were. It didn't matter whether she loved June or not. She was Jack's child, and for that reason alone, she would serve her daughter until the day she died. Well, the day *either* of them died, whichever came first. When June was happy, she was happy.

While Gertie normally kept these thoughts to herself, for some reason, she found herself explaining it to Bea in great detail. But she didn't judge her.

"You want to know a secret?" Bea whispered. "I didn't think I would love my kids either. Sometimes I wonder if I love them the way I should. You're not alone in that."

"I'm not?"

"I think every mom goes through that." She laid her head on Gertie's chest, closing her eyes. "You're not an evil monster for having those thoughts. Maybe you don't say it in words, but you do it in actions. You really love your daughter."

Some emotion stirred within Gertie, but she wasn't sure what it was. She found herself blinking back tears as she listened to the soothing words of her lover-enemy-girl-friend-nemesis, her voice sweet and rhythmic like all the mother's lullabies she never had.

# Chapter Ten

Within two weeks, Bea had boxed up her things, put her parents' home on the market, and moved in with Gertie and June. Each of the boys got their own rooms, something River showed endless gratitude for.

"I can't believe I can stretch out my arms and not touch the other wall in here," River crowed, eyes shining with wonder.

June and River became friends after they discovered they were both fans of some obscure children's book series. When June was home at night, she invited River to bake cookies and other sweet treats with her, and even helped him with his homework. A lonely and only child all her life, she was beyond eager to have a little brother. She was, however, *not* happy to be in forced proximity to Trevor.

Then again, no one was happy to be anywhere near that shit bag.

Each morning around the breakfast table, he was sure to voice his disdain and declare that various aspects of décor were some variation of an insert-homophobic-slur. The house was a cozy oasis until he arrived home, after which point, it erupted into a battlefield. A few weeks of this and Trevor somehow managed to grasp an ounce of a hint that everyone wanted him to stay as far away as possible. Gertie would only come across him at night, sneaking in through the back door. He never said anything, but glowered at her with a venomous expression.

By the second month of them living together, snow had fallen on the ground. Gertie only had until March before the election was held, and with the increasing pressure, she found herself more agitated as of late. Thankfully, Bea took on a lot of the household management duties so that she could focus on her campaign. There were letters to write, leaflets to design, speeches to make. Her game of revenge had effectively taken a backseat, perhaps—and here she promised herself she was only toying with the idea—permanently.

A few weekends before the holiday season, Bea took the kids to a Christmas tree farm the next town over, hoping to give Gertie a little time to herself to destress. Gertie spent it pacing about the house, trying to push through a bout of writer's block that had developed after she started writing her latest speech. She didn't get far before hearing a knock on the door downstairs. She descended the steps, watching as a man dressed all in black peered through the side window.

She opened the door. "Can I help you?"

He had a gaunt face, as sculpted as a mountain's peak, but his blistering blue eyes—and dark circles that would be the envy of raccoons everywhere—made him far less attractive. He scrubbed a gloved hand over his stubble and snorted, nostrils flaring wide enough that she noticed a hole in his deviated septum.

"Beatrice here?" His voice was gravel, chunky, grinding, and discordant to Gertie's ears.

"Bea?" It registered to Gertie at that moment who he was. Those half-moon eyes matched Trevor's. "You must be Westley."

"Righto." He didn't smile. He tilted his head back as if to take in the house once more, sighing with aggravation. "She did well for herself, huh?"

"I'm sorry?" Gertie's grip on the doorknob tightened. He casually placed a hand in the frame, above her head. She resisted the urge to crush his hand in it. The sound of his bones cracking would be more pleasant than the sound of his voice. "Are you here to drop off Christmas presents for the boys?"

"Not exactly." His eyes narrowed into slits. "Where's Bea?"

"She's with the kids."

"Where?"

"Why would I tell you that?"

"Because something very bad may happen to you if you don't."

"Really? What was your big plan here?" Gertie huffed.

"Taking my life back." He shoved Gertie backward, forcing himself through the open door. "You aware that your daughter has been tagging my boy on Instagram?"

River and June took a lot of photos together when they were baking. Cookies, cupcakes, candid selfies with their faces dusted in flour. She hadn't realized that someone could be spying on them. Hadn't realized that while Bea avoided social media to evade him, her children did not. To her knowledge, Westley lived several states away—the fact that he had driven God knows how far made him live up to the frightening stories Bea had told. Gertie didn't know if Bea had formally issued a restraining order, but she did know he had lost all custody.

"River's been doing well," Gertie said, backing away with caution. "Happier than ever."

"I'm sure you think so," Westley sneered, "but my boy isn't going to be raised by a fat fucking dyke."

Gertie sighed. This man was a carbon copy of Trevor, just with a liver that performed marginally worse. It was bad enough she had to suffer through that snot-nosed little shit's tirades. God, why were all the men in Bea's life so terrible? How had River become the only exception?

Boots still on, Westley stomped through the house and into the living room, a trail of slush and grimy snow following after him. He plopped onto the armchair and kicked his feet up on the coffee table, making himself at home. Gertie hovered over him, watching as the stains soaked into the carpet.

"What are you doing?" she asked, more confused than she was scared.

"I'm going to wait right here for my wife. Then I'm taking her. And if you try to stop me, I'll kick the shit out of you, and your pretty little daughter."

Gertie stared. "Are you high?"

"I'm the most sober I've been in six months," he replied, beaming with pride.

She sighed and retreated into the kitchen. This was *not* how she planned on spending her Saturday. She yanked open a drawer and grabbed a chef's knife, then looked back at the living room. He was still sitting there with a blissful unawareness of what she was planning.

No, not unaware. *Entitled.* Entitled to his ex-wife's body, a body Gertie had begun to relish exploring and lying next to each night. A body that Bea had whispered was hers and hers alone. A body that he had desecrated, over and over again. How long had Bea suffered with this pig sweating and grunting above her?

She put the knife back and picked up the meat cleaver instead, and headed back to the living room.

"Oink, oink, motherfucker," Gertie hissed, swinging it down on top of his head.

He cracked open like a piñata, brains and bits of blubber-lined skull splattering everywhere, on the chair, on the couch, on the carpet. She wrenched the cleaver out, blood guzzling out like one of those chocolate fountains they'd get for the annual holiday party, and she couldn't help but giggle at the sight of it.

Somehow still conscious, Westley staggered to his feet, roaring with rage. He swiped at her with a meaty paw, and she hacked at his hand, severing it between his ring and middle finger. It wilted like a scorned flower, hanging limp and useless in mid-air. He howled in rage, anguished tears springing to his eyes. He clutched it against his chest and attempted to lunge for her again, but he ended up toppling over the top of the armchair, which crashed to the ground with him. His free hand lunged forward and snapped up her ankle, sending her tumbling to the floor. Enraged, she screeched as the cleaver flew from her hands, spiraling across the wooden floor before stopping at the threshold of the kitchen.

Gertie shot a ferocious look in Westley's direction. He still had his grip on her ankle—his strength was surprising, considering he had half a brain and was bleeding out like a seal after a shark attack. With her free foot, she kicked him in the face as hard as she could, and shuddered in delight when she heard the crunch of the bones in his nose. He sobbed, swore, cussing her out with every misogynistic slur his swelling brain could muster. She dragged herself across the floor, wincing at the smarting pain in her hip, and he army-crawled after her—like a rabid dog on the hunt—leaving brushstrokes of blood in his place.

She grabbed the cleaver and rolled over to face him. He gripped the handle and wrestled with her for it with feeble hands. Gertie let one hand go and jammed it inside the cracked chestnut of his skull, her fingers coursing over the wrinkled folds of brain tissue and edges of bone, sharp like shards from a broken vase. He howled in pain, now trying to remove her hand. In that moment, she swung the cleaver forward again, striking him in his sharp-glass jaw, shattering it. The bone peeled away from the rest of his skull, the tattered strings of skin stretching to their limits as they struggled against the onslaught of blood. The bottom part of his tongue poked through the gory entrance, and Westley slurped on his blood, now unable to breathe.

With a sudden surge of enraged strength, she flung him back against the wooden floors and mounted him, cleaver held high above her head. She mashed it down into the crater of his face, over and over again, till his eyes became moldy berries floating in the raspberry jam of his brain. She carved and hacked into him long after his lungs had stopped struggling, cackling like a maniac, the gore soaking through the satin bathrobe Bea had bought her from Kohl's only a few weeks ago. Her tongue darted out of the corner of her mouth to lick a few stray droplets, and her chest heaved, trying to catch her breath.

As the adrenaline drifted from her body, so did her joy. She hung her head, sighing. She only hoped Earl made house calls.

The kids didn't ask too many questions when they came home to find that the couch and armchair were both missing. By that time, they'd mopped up the blood and bleached away every trace of Westley that had been in the house. Gertie explained she had made a pot of coffee, tripped, and spilled it everywhere, so she would have to replace the furniture. They bought the excuse, but they could've been easy to persuade because of the excitement of a tree. It had been years since River and Trevor had a proper Christmas. Even the surly teenage boy couldn't help but smile as he hung an ornament from one of its branches.

Bea perched herself on Gertie's lap, a strand of mistletoe pinched between two fingers. Gertie smiled, her heart fluttering in her chest. She offered Bea a chaste kiss, wrapping her arms around the waist whose curves and dips she had long since memorized. Bea's laughter left her mouth in a whisper, and she pressed herself possessively against Gertie.

"Have you thought about what you want for Christmas?" Bea whispered into Gertie's ear.

Gertie chuckled, "I don't need anything."

"It doesn't have to be a material gift," Bea teased. "It could be...a request."

"*Beatrice.*"

"They're not listening to us," Bea chuckled, watching as the kids playfully discussed decorating the tree. "You know, I ought to thank you for this. The boys really...*really* needed a normal Christmas this year. Well, as normal as it could be."

"You don't have to thank me for anything."

After all, it had been Gertie's plan. She watched as Trevor circled the tree with a strand of tinsel, almost elbowing June in the process. He glanced down at his squabbling pseudo-sister, and there was something in his eyes—some sort of expression—that Gertie did not like. She squeezed Bea a little tighter and pressed her forehead against the back of her neck, inhaling the scent of pine that lingered over her body. She could worry about Trevor later. This was a happy family moment, a desire she had once yearned for but had long suppressed.

"I wanted to show you something I got today," Bea urged her, squeezing her hand. "Come with me for a sec?"

Gertie nodded, following her upstairs to their shared bedroom. Bea's eager hands locked the door behind her, then threw her arms around her neck, her mouth hungrily meeting hers. Her kiss felt a little sloppy, almost drunk, but when Gertie looked at her face, her gray eyes were clear, and her mouth was swollen.

"Sorry," Bea whispered. "I just really wanted you to fuck me."

Gertie removed her glasses. "So no surprise?"

"Oh! No, I do have that."

She gestured to the bed, indicating that Gertie should wait there. She complied, and reached into the top drawer of the nightstand to retrieve the strap-on along with the steak knife she hadn't bothered to return to the kitchen. Bea exited the closet, topless, clad in a pair of crotchless black boy shorts. Gertie laughed.

"You don't like it?" Bea asked, self-conscious.

"No, it's just kinda…funny. Unexpected," Gertie told her.

Bea pouted. "I can take it off."

"Get your ass over here," Gertie ordered. "Let me see it."

Reluctant, Bea shuffled over to her, still upset. Gertie squeezed her hand and spun her around, examining it closer. It was the most feminine thing Bea owned, but her muscular ass looked damn great in those shorts.

"It was supposed to be your Christmas present," Bea said. "But I thought it would be fun to reveal it tonight."

"It's nice."

"If you don't like it, I can return it."

Gertie laughed again, pulling her onto her lap. She cupped Bea's face in her hands and shook her head. "I love it. You look hot. I just thought if either of us was going to wear lingerie, it would be *me*. I didn't think this was in your comfort zone."

"It's not. But you *are* my comfort zone." Bea locked her arms around her neck. "I want to do nice things for you sometimes too, y'know?"

"You do nice things for me all the time."

"Unloading the dishwasher before I go to work is the bare minimum, Gert."

"I hate doing it!" Gertie smiled, shrugging her shoulders. "And I'm not talking about that. You gave me an afternoon off. I didn't even have to ask, but you knew I needed it."

For some reason, tears welled in Bea's eyes. She hugged Gertie tight, choking back a sob. Gertie rubbed her back in gentle, circular motions.

"You're always—you always know exactly what to say when I need it."

"I'm sorry I laughed. Let me make it up to you," Gertie said into her ear. She delivered a resounding slap to Bea's ass, and felt the woman's body shudder in turn. "Stop fucking crying."

Bea's eyes glazed over in a lustful haze, and Gertie watched as her chest heaved with each breath. Her fingers slipped inside of her, trying to stretch her enough to take in the dick.

"Tight," Gertie commented. "You're gonna need to prep this dick well." Bea leaned over to the nightstand as if to retrieve a bottle of lube, but Gertie grabbed her hair and pulled her back. "Nope. Suck it."

Bea crouched down in front of her and opened her mouth wide. She kept her eyes on Gertie as her tongue swirled around the head, lapping at the tip. Gertie grabbed her head and shoved it down hard, forcing her to deep-throat it. Bea moaned as Gertie thrust into her mouth.

"You want this cock inside you?"

Bea's fingers reached down to stroke herself in response. Gertie pushed her away, then pulled the woman onto her lap, entering her with force. Bea winced, her voice catching in her throat, and Gertie thrust into her, slamming her hips upwards.

"Oh fuck," Bea whimpered, slumping over Gertie's shoulders. "Oh my God..."

Gertie lay flat back against the bed, panting from exertion. She kept her hands on Bea's waist as she rolled her hips forward. Bea's breasts bounced up and down with wild abandon. Gertie continued to move her hips, trying to match her rhythm.

"You like that, whore?"

Bea's moan left her mouth in a whimper, her movements becoming desperate. Already, her body was drenched in sweat. Gertie's fingers reached up to tweak her nipples, and she yelped, her voice an inordinate high pitch, a sign that she would come soon.

"I asked you a fucking question."

"Y-yes," Bea gasped. "I love it."

"You like it when I destroy your pussy?"

"Yes," she purred.

Her fingers stretched upward, embedding themselves in her hair, her cries primal and desperate. Gertie squeezed her thighs, both to excite her as well as help her maintain her balance. What a sight. Bea, her entire body, red and glistening with sweat, drool accumulating at the corners of her mouth. Gertie's hips continued to grind against her, but she knew she couldn't come like this. Bea needed a little more violence.

So Gertie slapped her. Gasping, Bea fell to the side, stunned, legs twitching. Before she could right herself, Gertie spread open her legs, and forced inside her, pressing down with all her weight. She placed a hand against her throat, applying pressure, but careful not to cut off her air supply. She slammed into her, grunting from the effort. Bea's eyes rolled into the back of her head and her tongue hung from her mouth, groaning. Seeing that she was close, Gertie reached for the knife, and pressed the hilt of it against her throat, the blade turned away from Bea's skin.

Her voice lowered to a menacing growl. "Tell me this

is *my* pussy."

"*Ahn*—i-it's yours."

"It's my *what?*"

"*Ugh*—*ahh-ah!* Your pussy, oh, oh *fuck!*"

Bea's body tightened around the dick in a vice-like grip as her hands twisted in the sheets. Her voice reached its peak. Tantalizing tremors coursed through her shaking legs, and Gertie watched the spectacle of Bea's orgasm.

She removed her hand, dropped the knife, and collapsed beside her, sweating. Bea was blissed out, her eyes dreamlike. Her hand rubbed herself more, trying to capture the fading pleasures that ebbed from her body.

"Good?" Gertie asked.

Bea's eyes sparkled. "Beyond good."

"I didn't slap you too hard, right?" She rubbed the tender mark on Bea's face with a gentle hand.

"Unless there's blood coming out or you break my nose, I don't think you could slap me too hard." She rolled over to face Gertie, kissing her, nipping at her bottom lip. "I meant what I said, you know."

Gertie chuckled, "I'm sure you did."

"I mean it." Bea gripped Gertie's hand, placing it between her legs. She was soaking wet. "You could rip me apart from the inside out, and I would love every second of it."

"Mmm…" Gertie licked her bottom lip, trying to catch her breath between kisses. "If you want more tonight,

I'm going to need a minute."

"Take several minutes," Bea replied, undoing the clasps that held the strap-on in place around her waist. "I'll get you warmed up again."

Gertie felt her clit throb in response, and she lay back against the pillows. Bea set the strap-on to the side and, licking her lips, lay down so she could bury her face between her legs. Sweet God, this woman was ravenous.

"Bea?"

Bea pulled away. "Yeah?"

"You…" Gertie's chest heaved, and she bit her lip when she felt Bea's fingers slip inside her. "You should buy lingerie more often."

That night, Bea thought she had given Gertie an early Christmas present. But what she didn't realize is that Gertie had given her one too—it was just being pulverized in an industrial-sized mulching machine back on Earl's property.

When a couple weeks had passed into the new year, it became clear to Westley's vagabond friends back in Kentucky that the bastard had gone missing. Bea was questioned, along with her sons, but none of them had heard from him in a long time. Earl had disposed of the body along with the vehicle, and the man was in too much credit card debt to pay for things with anything other than cash, so there was no evidence he had ever been at the Burns' household.

Perhaps if they bothered to check *any* traffic cams, they could've pinpointed that he was in Appledale. But the cops weren't too eager to invest effort in a man who had known ties to loan sharks, and a rap sheet full of assault and domestic violence charges. Westley was a bastard through and through, and he would not be missed, least of all by River and Bea, who had suffered the most from his aggression.

But Trevor did grieve. He spiraled into these long fits where he wasn't sobbing so much as he was howling. Death metal music often accompanied these outbursts which would rattle the walls and disrupt everyone's peace. He became more aggressive than before, and instead of insulting people with a barrage of slurs, would smash things against the wall. Family photos? Bam. Ceramic Tupperware? Smashed. Carpets? Shredded with a kitchen knife. Bea and Gertie would come home from political functions to find the house in a complete state of disarray. No amount of grounding, privilege-revoking, or Bea's enraged screeching sessions could stop this boy from behaving at his very worst.

Tensions in the house were running higher than ever, especially with election right around the corner. Gertie couldn't tell the little pissant what she really wanted to say, not when Bea was within earshot all the time. It caused her to build up rage that affected her even in her sleep. Bea would shake her awake in the middle of the night if she was grinding her jaw too hard. She had to buy a mouthguard at CVS. There were only a few more formal functions left to attend before the election, and while Gertie was a surefire choice, she couldn't afford to be cocky. She had already made too many impulsive decisions this past year.

With shaking hands, Gertie stared into the mirror and tried to loop her earring through. Bea, already dressed in her tux, brushed up behind her and helped her.

"I've already told him that he has to be out of the house tonight," Bea told her. "I've got the security camera alerts set up on my phone, so I'll know if he comes back earlier than he's supposed to."

"Odd to think that we're trying to tell him to stay *away* from home, instead of staying in."

"When he's destroyed this much stuff, I don't think we have any other choice. It's not safe, but I'm tired of cleaning it up," Bea sighed. "I don't know what the next step is after this. A psychiatric evaluation?"

"Might be necessary." Gertie applied lipstick as she spoke, careful to trace just her lips and not the skin. "Could be oppositional defiant disorder."

"Hell, with his dad's genes, he could've inherited anything," Bea grumbled.

Tonight there was a soirée at Joanna's, a final attempt to connect with voters in a large social setting. After this, it was only town halls and canvassing. The past few months had been so chaotic that she scarcely had a moment to catch her breath. Since killing Westley, she had almost this permanent tightness in her chest. Perhaps it was the guilt from slaughtering both Bea's parents and her ex-husband. Could've also been the anxiety from knowing that June's junior prom was right around the corner—yet another reminder that her baby bird would soon fly from the nest.

Whatever it was, Gertie had to fight to suppress all her negative emotions. At the party, she helped herself to a few too many glasses of champagne and relied on Bea to carry on most of the conversations. Now intoxicated, she could laugh more, mingle more, breathe more. She could even stand to talk to Misty, whom she still loathed with a passion.

"How're you doing in the polls, Gert? I forget who you were even up against."

"Dick Harding."

"That's right. How unfortunate. You'd think he wouldn't go by Dick," Misty said with a smirk. "And how've things been with the girlfriend since moving in together?"

"Good."

"Yeah?" Misty's finger circled the rim of her glass. "I saw the photos June posted on Instagram. Bea's kid is real cute. What's his name?"

"River."

"River. Yeah. He's sweet." She took a sip, releasing a

satisfied *pahh.* "Those boys have been through a lot in the past six months, haven't they?"

Gertie nodded, unsure where this conversation was going. She searched for Bea in the crowd and spotted her by the banquet table. When she tried to excuse herself, Misty interjected with another trademark shady comment.

"It's interesting that so many bad things happened to Bea and her kids after she met you."

Gertie looked back at Misty, perplexed. "What?"

Misty shrugged her shoulders. Her smile was smarmy with intoxication, but her eyes were as clear as glass. "Just saying. It's tragic."

"I don't—I mean, it is, but I don't know what you're implying. It's like you're suggesting that I'm..."

Misty guffawed, touching a hand against her chest, as if she thought it was so precious. "Oh my god, darling, I'm not accusing you of something flagrant. Her parents died in a car accident. I'm more so talking about the dad."

"What about him?"

"Oh come on, Gertie, you *know,*" she giggled. "Everyone else may have forgotten, but I sure haven't. Who was it—Dorothea. *Dorothea.*"

Gertie stood there, stiff, each limb in her body turning to rusted iron in desperate need of oil. She glanced in Bea's direction, trying to send out an SOS, but she was shooting the shit with some other lady by the crab dip. *Damn it.*

"Dorothea was the one whose husband you dug up dirt on, right? You hired the P.I. to get the photos of the mistress, didn't you?"

"I don't know what you're talking about."

Misty bit her tongue between her teeth in a delighted smile. She rolled her eyes. "Whatever you say." She whisked around the dwindling liquid in her glass, dissatisfied. "From the rumors, Bea's ex-husband was a bad egg. I'm sure whatever you said—or did—made him go away for good."

"I've never met Westley," Gertie said, her voice taut with anger.

*This stupid bitch. What the hell is she implying? Why is she always on my case?* It wasn't like Dorothea was even a *good* PTA president. Her husband wasn't going to stay faithful to her even if Gertie hadn't hired the escort. The man was the equivalent of a dog begging for a bone before dinner. Nothing Gertie had done back then was bad, as Dorothea's life would've been dismantled with or without her involvement. The woman needed a push to get the hell out of her way, and that's all it was.

As for Westley, well he needed a push into the next lifetime so he would stop torturing the woman who had escaped him. By taking him out, she had done swaths of women a favor. Gertie was no meddling ninny. She was a goddamn hero, a servant to her community. It was high fucking time that Misty stopped acting like she was anything else. Knowing this asshole, she was probably blabbing about that Dorothea story to anyone who listened. She had long been an annoyance, but now?

She was officially a risk.

And Gertie couldn't have any more of those.

Gertie's head was so full of anger that she tuned out the rest of the conversation. Misty said something in her slurred voice and wandered off. Gertie followed her a safe distance behind, keeping her shoulders relaxed and smiling at those she passed by.

Misty was so drunk she could barely stand on those ugly fucking kitten heels. *Cheap bitch.* Those were the same ones she had worn to the Parents' Night. They didn't even match her tacky fuchsia dress. She traipsed after Misty, following her down the back hallway that led to the kitchen. Full glasses of champagne waited to replenish the drunk partygoers. Gertie slipped into the room and pulled the door shut. Misty paid her no mind and picked up one of the glasses.

"I'd like you to not spread rumors about me," Gertie said.

Misty scoffed. "Please. Anything that comes out of my mouth has been borrowed from at least a dozen people already."

"I thought we were friends?" Gertie pressed. "Why does it seem like lately you've done nothing but make shitty comments?"

"Friends? That's a laugh, Gertrude. You aren't friends with people. You use people."

"*Use* people?"

"You use Bea, you use the PTA ladies, you use your daughter—I'm sorry, no, you *live* through your daughter. Now we're just suddenly supposed to believe that you've turned a new leaf and are doing things for yourself?"

"I do what's *best* for June, Misty. Just as you do what's best for your kids."

"*My* kids are not my entire life." She swayed on her feet. "They aren't my only source of happiness. And I wouldn't take other people down to make sure they got ahead."

Gertie stared at her. "Then I don't think you're as good a mother as you think you are."

"Fuck you," Misty spat, eyes thinning with rage. "Who are you to tell me that, you fat fucking asshole?"

"Is that *really* all the best anyone can do to insult me?" Gertie cried out, frustrated. "Seriously, I—it's more annoying than it is hurtful. At least my fat ass is getting laid, Misty, your husband hasn't touched you in months. And that's even *after* he started taking Viagra."

Misty's voice lowered into a growl that accelerated into a screech—the engine of an F-1 spinning out on the racetrack. She threw the liquid into Gertie's face, smearing the mascara on her eyes. With a focused calmness, Gertie wiped it away. Misty hovered over her, doing her best to be menacing.

"Quit pretending like that little bull dyke would love you if you hadn't rescued her from the street. You're pathetic, Gert. You're really pathetic."

"The only one pathetic here is you." Gertie tilted her head to the side. "You think I'm shallow and superficial, Misty? I suggest you take a good, long, hard look at yourself in the mirror. I may be the richest woman in town, but I'm not spending all my money on plastic surgeries and Cabo vacations and the latest designer clothes to fill the void left by a husband who won't fuck me. If you think I'm a shell of a human being because of how I dedicated so much of my life to my daughter, well, it's better than being a vapid bottle-baby like yourself."

"Why you…"

"You know what I've learned from dealing with mean girls like you? They're sad. They're sad because they want someone who will love them despite all their flaws. But they're so shallow that they will *never* have that. They will *never* have that unconditional love. Bea and Jack—they love me despite the thickness of my thighs, the bloat of my belly, the rolls of fat on my ass. Actually, no, not in spite of, but *because* of. They worship me. And while I'm getting my pussy eaten out three times in a row, you're at home bemoaning the fact that you've built a life for yourself that you hate.

"Well, I don't feel sorry for you, and it isn't my fault that you'll live and die in mediocrity. The only way out at this point is to kill yourself, but you're too much of a drunk and a coward to ever be successful at that."

To her credit, Misty didn't waste a breath. She cracked the glass against Gertie's face, the shards splintering into her cheek. Gertie stood there, her eyes boring holes into Misty. The woman stammered, aghast, terrified by her lackluster response.

"Oh Misty," Gertie whispered. "You're going to regret that."

Gertie reached a trembling hand up to her cheek, feigning a whimpering that grew into a screech of pain. She staggered backward—

—out the door she had so carefully blocked.

Now surrounded by others, Gertie increased the dramatics. Wailing, she collapsed to her knees and others rushed to surround her. Stupefied, Misty stumbled out after her, the shattered glass still in hand. Droplets of Gertie's blood glistened on the edge of it.

"Excuse me! Excuse me!" Bea pushed through the crowd and collapsed by Gertie's side.

Someone in the crowd offered Gertie a cloth napkin, which she pressed against her cheek. It quickly dampened with blood. Bea's ferocious eyes widened and she glared at Misty.

"What the fuck is wrong with you?" Bea snarled, teeth bared.

Gertie sobbed. "She—she wasn't walking straight, so

I tried to help her, and she attacked me. Ow, ow, ow, oh my god, it hurts so bad!"

Bea hugged Gertie to her chest. A couple of bystanders surrounded Misty, who shrieked in fear, trying to evade their grasp. She only made things worse for herself. The more she resisted, the more others tried to grab her. To Gertie, she looked like that little rabbit she found that day in the garden, desperate to escape a pack of wolves. She wished that's what she was witnessing—the evisceration of Misty limb from bloody limb, torn into a useless steaming carcass that would collapse at her feet. But not all of her villains' lives could end in bloodshed. Sometimes they were stupid enough to ruin themselves.

Devastated that her party was ruined, Joanna sobbed when the police officers whisked Misty away. Paramedics tended to Gertie's wounds, but she did not press charges. On her campaign pages, she acknowledged the incident but declared herself as a purveyor of peace, wanting only for Misty to seek treatment for alcoholism.

Now while the public lauded Gertie for her kindness toward Misty, they themselves were not so kind to her. A few more weeks and her kids couldn't go to Trinity without relentless bullying for their mother being a floozy. Like Dorothea, Misty was left with little choice but to retreat from the PTA altogether, and at the order of a judge, was forced to go to rehab.

Out of sight, and now—*finally*—out of her mind.

# Chapter Eleven

Less than a year ago, Gertie drove around town alone, drifting from one destination to the next. Now almost every day, she had someone to entertain her with car ride karaoke and accompany her on spontaneous stops at McDonald's. Like today, after Bea had begged her for an ice cream cone off the dollar menu, even though it was the dead of winter. Gertie helped herself to one as well. The cashier recognized her from the school board posters and wished her luck on her campaign. Ice cream in hand, the two pulled into a parking spot in the near-empty lot, a lineup of cars proceeding at a snails pace behind them.

Bea licked the tip of the cone, a delighted smile on her face. "I swear, they have better soft serve here than Dairy Queen."

"If you think that, I think it's been a *long* time since you've been to Dairy Queen." But it *was* damn good. "Maybe that could be another trip sometime this week. I've been craving an Oreo Blizzard."

"You sure? I know how busy you've been. I want you to focus on winning the election."

"Bea," she mumbled through a mouthful of sweetness, "I've got this in the bag. Don't worry."

It was true. She was performing better in the polls than ever before—her opponent couldn't hope to achieve the numbers that she had. Then again, he spent more time fundraising while Gertie had paid for the whole campaign with her own money. The PTA was so sure of her victory that they'd begun workshopping who the next president would be. At this stage, the unfortunate decision was Kellyanne. Once she won the election, she knew things would slow down, but for now, she had to keep Bea happy with little things like this. It didn't take long to bring a smile to her face, and god, how Gertie had fallen in love with that smile.

Bea planted a creamy kiss against her cheek. "That's right, baby."

"Once this is all over, before my term starts, I'd like to take us on a trip."

"Really? Where would you want to go?"

"You tell me." Gertie grinned. That *I-Love-Lucy* shocked expression on Bea's face was adorable. "You want to go home and throw a dart at a globe, we can do it."

"We don't own a globe, and I can't throw for shit," Bea

giggled.

"Well, I'm partial to sipping daiquiris on a beach somewhere. Lisbon, Martha's Vineyard, Fiji."

"Gert, those are not simple vacation destinations. Those are for honeymoons."

"I've never had a honeymoon." She and Jack couldn't afford one back then.

"Neither did I, unless you count the one night Westley and I spent in a Thunderbird when we went to visit his father in South Dakota." Bea shuddered at the memory. "I will be happy anywhere you decide to take me. But we couldn't go without the kids."

"Why not?" As soon as she said it, she knew the answer. *Trevor. Shit.*

There was no way they could leave June and River alone with that animal. At times like these, she almost wished she hadn't killed the Robinsons or Westley. Maybe if she had kept them alive, she could've peddled the kid off on them. She and Bea had looked into military schools, but they only accepted those in good academic standing, and even *if* Trevor had that, there was the issue of shipping him to a different state altogether, since there were no institutions like that in Ohio. He could ditch at any point along the way, and wreak havoc somewhere else. There were "behavioral schools", but if they weren't careful with their choices, they could end up enrolling him in a place that utilized wilderness therapy, a practice which had come under fire as of late. He had to go, but he wasn't going to go anytime soon. In the meantime,he was on the fast-track for a juvie sentence, and while he wasn't on the public radar right now, by the time she was up for reelection, his antics would no doubt smear her public image.

When they finished their ice cream, they sped off for home. They discovered the garage was open, and the trash can was scorched, like someone had built a fire in it. Droplets of green plastic stained the cracked cement floor. Collectively, the women breathed a sigh of frustration, their bodies tensing at the sight.

Trevor had skipped school yet again.

"Goddamn it." Bea swung open the door. "I'm going to smack him senseless."

As much as Bea threatened physical violence, she never followed through, even though Gertie wished she would. Gertie parked the car along the side of the garage and inspected the damage. Yep, there was something blackened resting at the bottom of the bin, and the entire thing reeked like ash and…flesh. *Flesh?* She sniffed again. *No. Chicken? No.*

A bird. There was a dead bird resting atop the newspapers, its feathers melted against its fragile skull, its little legs severed clean off—gardening shears, judging by the pair only a few inches away from the trash can. Her stomach churned, and she closed the lid. She could hear Bea screeching at her son inside the house. No matter how many times they punished or grounded this little shit, he wouldn't relent. Even more infuriating, he wasn't afraid of them. Sometimes he had the nerve to wear a little smug smirk on his face.

Today was one of those days.

River and June arrived home around the same time, bearing witness to the nasty argument. Bea sent Trevor to his room, then left to take River to soccer practice. June started her homework in the kitchen, and Gertie retreated upstairs to catch up on some TV and do some campaign-related work. June didn't like it when she watched TV in the same room that she was doing homework, she found the noise distracting. She listened to the sounds of Trevor smashing and banging things around in his room, as he was wont to do during his tantrums.

When the noises dissipated, that was when she heard it. The soft *squeak* of the doorknob turning. Footsteps padding down the stairs. Tension returned to her shoulders, and she listened to the murmurings of her daughter speaking to him. His nasty little replies—she couldn't make out the words, but she knew he was being gross. A gasp. Another gasp. Something being knocked over. Gertie sighed and turned off the TV, then shuffled downstairs to investigate.

June had toppled over backward in her chair, and Trevor had climbed on top of her, pinning one wrist to the floor. His other hand covered her mouth, smothering her screams. Tears burned in the corners of her eyes, and she looked to her mother, pleading. Enraged, Gertie roared and threw Trevor off June. She began kicking and smacking him, hitting him square in the ears. Disoriented, Trevor howled in pain and clutched his head, trying to avoid her violence. June scrambled off the floor and raced out of the house, wailing.

Gertie pointed a stiff finger at Trevor. "Don't you move off that fucking floor."

She followed June, who was getting into her Honda Civic.

"I can't stay here, Mommy. I can't." June choked on her tears, rolling down the window. "Not with that monster in the house."

"I know," Gertie whispered. Unbelievable hurt washed over her, followed by a sense of relief. Bea was right. She really did love June. "I'll handle it, okay? Do you have someone's place you can go to?"

June nodded, wiping away her tears. "Tanya's."

Gertie leaned over and kissed her daughter's forehead. "Call me before you go to sleep tonight."

"O-okay." But June didn't move. Her face was twisted in shame and confusion, the tears continuing to fall. "What did I—why would he do that to me, Mom?"

"Because there's something *wrong* with him, June."

She had known this for a long time, but she had compared Trevor's threat level to that of a rat: a disgusting nuisance with a potential for damage. It was time to start thinking of Trevor for what he really was. A rabid dog. Dangerous, and willing to bite.

But Gertie could bite back harder, and she had bigger teeth.

After June pulled out of the driveway, Gertie wandered back in the house. A mosaic of shards littered the floor at Trevor's feet. He ransacked the cabinets for another plate and shattered it on the floor.

"This has gone on long enough," Gertie shouted at him over the din of the smashing. "Property damage is one thing, but assaulting my daughter?"

Trevor stopped, breathless, red in the face. "I'm gonna break as much shit as it takes to get her to leave you. Whatever you think you're building together, I'll break."

Gertie scrunched up her nose. "That kind of symbolism is better received in a college level art course."

Trevor's hand clenched around a mug, but this time, he didn't throw it. He stood there, panting, his eyes red but not dripping tears. *Oh. That's what this emotion is.* All along they thought it was rage, but it was sadness. Grief. Gertie was familiar with grief.

And she knew how to manipulate the grieving.

"I know things have been hard." She approached him slowly, tiptoeing around the mess on the floor. "Especially with your dad being gone."

"Dad would *never* leave me."

He set the mug on the counter, then buried his face in

his hands. At last, the tears began to fall. He sobbed, a wrenching, awful sound like water squeaking from a rusty faucet.

"I'm sure he didn't mean to."

He *clearly* didn't. Had he gotten what he wanted that day, he probably would have killed them all in a murder suicide. At best, would've returned to using River's arms as an ashtray and smacking Bea around in the dead of night. It was no life for any of them.

But Trevor was like his father. Pigheaded to the point that he took his own stubbornness as fact. His dad was a great person to him because he was incapable of critical thinking and taking evidence into account. Here he was whining about how no one saw his pain, when he refused to see his mother's or his brother's.

"I just want this nightmare to end."

*So do I,* Gertie thought. *So do I.*

As it turns out, if you put your mind to it, gaining the trust of a troubled teenage boy is quite easy. They're like stray dogs. You feed them a little bit of kindness and they will follow. Gertie comforted the piss-baby until she felt like she could ask him to go for a ride with her. Told him they could take a walk and "get some of this energy out". Along the way she drove slower than normal, taking her time, letting him pick out his favorite choice of music and suffering through two Nine Inch Nails songs. She knew where to go, though, and how far she could go before she had to stop. Once you got to the parking lot of Trinity Oaks, there were security cameras. But the little road leading to the school? As good as desolate.

She pulled alongside the shoulder, staring up at the massive building looming in the distance, the spires of its individual towers piercing the squashed-blueberry sky. She didn't have too much time before Bea and River got home. And she still had to figure out what to do for dinner tonight.

Trevor hopped out of the truck before she had to tell him to do it. "Here?"

Gertie nodded. "There's a river. It's nice."

She reached into the back of the truck, behind the driver's seat, and picked up her purse, along with a dog leash that she kept in case she found a stray or two in need of assistance. She tucked it underneath her wallet, out of sight, and locked the truck before leading him down the steep pathway. Snow and sticks crunched beneath their boots. The trees may have lost all of their leaves, but Gertie was thankful that the branches were thick enough to hide them from the main road.

She pretended to listen to Trevor bemoan the deaths of his grandparents and the disappearance of his father. Her eyes focused on the hills, scanning for any over-eager hikers or God forbid, one of those skeletal high-on-life runners that always stomped around no matter the weather. She had to keep looking because if she stared at him for too long, she was worried he would see the look of disgust scrawled across her face. When they got to the river bed, they stopped. Gertie crouched at the surface of the navy-blue waters, peering into it, not a thing staring back. In the summers, this river was as shiny as a polished sapphire but in the overcast light, it resembled a deep grave. Slow-melting ice flowed drifted by. It was peaceful, but not for very much longer.

"What're you looking at?"

"Sometimes you can see turtles down here."

"*Turtles?*"

"Yeah," Gertie said. "And little river fish. They're silver, glimmering, kinda pretty."

"Dad used to take me fishing when we'd visit Rapid Valley." Trevor crouched down beside her. "I always thought I'd go back there with him one day. Maybe after I graduated."

"Maybe you still can," Gertie muttered. *In the afterlife, that is.* "Oh! I think I saw a fish there."

"Really?"

She wanted to laugh. This was too easy.

One little push against his back and the boy tumbled into the river, face first. The coldness of the water shocked him, and while he struggled to upright himself, she whipped the leash out of her purse. Leaning over, she tightened it around his neck; he was still submerged, screams escaping his mouth in bubbles as he thrashed and thrashed. He was strong, but she knew he wouldn't last long in these temperatures. Hell, she had to be careful not to injure herself. Even her gloved hands were getting chilled from the waters, and if she had to go for much longer, they would go numb. When he stopped after a minute or so, she let go of the leash, and tucked it into the pocket of her sweatshirt. His body bobbed in the water, rolling over almost in slow motion, and part of his face crested above the surface. Those eyes that had stared at her with such malice were now empty.

*Finally.*

But she couldn't even enjoy it. *Shit.* She didn't think this one through.

She had killed him in the shallow end of the bank, so if she wanted him to drift downstream, she would have to wade in and push him, and it was far too cold to do that. Since his neck was covered in strangulation marks, even if she did let him drift down the river, someone would suspect foul play upon his inevitable resurfacing.

She stood and brushed some mud and snow from her damp jeans, then retrieved her purse. She sighed, and with shaking hands, reached into her purse to dial Earl. He picked up on the third ring.

"Hey. Got another one for you." The line was silent for a moment, so she spoke again, more urgent this time. "Hello? Did you hear me? I have another one for you. Another—*plant* to take care of, or whatever."

"You gotta be shitting me," he sighed. "Where're you at?"

"The riverside by Trinity Oaks."

"You're at your daughter's *school?*"

"Yes. Can you meet me here?"

"Gimme fifteen minutes."

Those felt like the longest minutes of Gertie's life. She sat on a snow-blanketed rock and contemplated all of her choices. Anyone could have come by. *Anyone.* But if she made it through this, it would be the last time. The last time she would ever take another life. No matter how delicious it felt, she would never do it again.

There was too much at stake now.

Earl wandered down the hill not much later than when he told her he would. His face twisted in confusion when he saw the body lying in the water, pinned between a few of the rocks.

"Is that a kid?"

"My girlfriend's kid."

"Your—good Lord."

"He tried to assault my daughter."

"That explains it. But what do you want me to do about it?"

"Get rid of the body?"

"You want me to haul a 175-pound boy up this here hill?"

"Unless you have any better ideas?"

He stroked his beard. "How'd you kill him?"

She held up the leash.

He winced. "Strangled him? You left marks?" he whispered, his voice hushed and angry. "You're asking me to do the impossible, woman."

"Hey, I'm paying you, aren't I?"

"It's not the money that's the problem. It's the body. It's the setup. How do you explain this?"

"He was…troubled. Deeply troubled. Troubled teens run away from home all the time."

"Not without leaving a note." He frowned, crossing his arms.

"A *note*? This kid barely passed English last term. I doubt he wrote much of anything."

"He's a teenager, teens are melodramatic. They need the attention, so we need the note. Do you have any handwriting of his?"

"Hmmm. You could check his wallet. See if he's got notes in there. Otherwise, I'd have to snoop in his room, but I can't do that right now."

He shook his head. "You really fucked this up, Gert."

"Just…do what you can with the body. I don't think we'll worry if he goes 'missing' for a couple of days before finding the note. Like I said, he was a real piece of work."

Earl glared. "Sounds like you had something in common."

"What's your fucking problem?"

"You're asking me to cut up a kid."

"I didn't realize that's how your absurd moral compass operated, Batman. Cut me a break. He's the last one, okay?"

"Good. Because I don't clean up after serial killers."

Gertie set her jaw. "I'll wire you the money tonight."

"Don't do that. It's the dead of winter. If you get audited, no one will believe your gardener was working right now. I'll have to come up with something and send you the invoice."

He squatted down and dragged the body from the water. Trevor's skin was now ashy and gray, a cloudy twilight that would never see the sun again. His body was rather stiff, and whether that was from rigor mortis or the freezing waters, Gertie didn't know. She took one last look at the boy to soak it all in before marching back up the pathway, onward to her warm and cozy home, where his mother was waiting for her.

And she *still* had to make dinner.

# Chapter Twelve

As Gertie had told Earl, no one asked any questions. She explained to Bea that there had been an argument and that June had fled, followed by Trevor not long after. She rummaged through his room until she could find a sufficient handwriting sample to send to Earl. Within two days his runaway letter showed up in the mailbox, after Bea had gone to work. The mothers did their due diligence in reporting him to the police as a runaway, but as with Westley, they were not invested in finding him. Gertie advised her publicist of the matter, who worked to keep it quiet. Trevor wouldn't so much as be a photograph on a carton of milk.

Yet Gertie hadn't received her invoice. She called Earl a couple of times, only to be forwarded to voicemail. Each day she religiously combed through their mail. She tried to suppress her worrying by assuring herself that he was just on vacation. Old men like him were snowbirds, the type to seek solace in some place like Myrtle Beach. *The beach, the beach.* Now that Trevor was gone, she could take Bea there. Sun, sex, and shadowy walks along the edge of sunset.

Earl resurfaced a week before the election. He arrived at the house not long after Bea left for work. When Gertie opened the door to let him inside, she wasn't scared at all. Rather, she was delighted to see him.

"Did you get it taken care of?"

His mouth pressed into a grim line. "Yep."

"And the body?"

"Got a friend at a crematorium who owed me a favor. No part of him will ever resurface."

"Good, good."

"Except for this."

Earl reached into his back pocket and withdrew a single digit, which had been sliced off at the second knuckle. It was tiny and pruny, like a moldy piece of fruit that had gotten stuck at the bottom of the sink after washing the dishes. The nail was stubby, albeit pretty intact, as were the squiggly lines of Trevor's fingerprints.

Evidence.

"What are you doing?" Gertie asked, confused. She plugged her nose and resisted the urge to gag at the smell of rot wafting from the gory souvenir. "Why would you keep that?"

"I think you know why. I need to get my fair cut."

She spread her hands. "I've been waiting on the invoice like you told me to. It's not like I've been skipping out."

"I figured you might if I told you my price."

"Shoot."

"Fifty."

"Million?" Gertie whispered, eyes widening. She tugged at her gold necklace, suddenly feeling like her throat was constricting. "I'm rich, but not *that* rich."

"I know your net worth."

"That is almost the *entirety* of my fortune. Why would you ask for that much? It's not like someone else is offering you that kind of pay for dirt on a school board member."

"No, but you did make me chop up a kid, Gertie. And I'm not sure if you knew this, but I don't quite like you."

"Well, I know that *now*. Fifty million. Fifty million, Jesus Christ."

"If you won't pay that price for your freedom, then what about the life of your girlfriend?"

"Bea? I started this whole thing to drive her to the brink of insanity. I would…" Gertie trailed off.

Flashes of her face flipped through the photograph album of her mind. Heat rose on her body from the places that Bea had caressed with love and passion and desire. She hadn't fully realized it until now, but her game of revenge had ended a long time ago. She lost, but ended up winning more than she could ever have hoped for.

And this bearded Billy Bob Thornton knockoff was here to take it all away.

"You and I both know how much you love that woman. So cut the shit and we'll talk business, okay? No one has to get hurt here."

Except he did.

Because just as much as Gertie didn't want to deal with the consequences of her actions, she also didn't want to pay for them. After all, she quite liked being rich. She led him through the house, into the kitchen, and offered him a seat at the dining room table. She noticed his shoulders stiffen, as if fearful.

*Good.* Fear was good.

Knowing how clean and quiet he wanted to be, Gertie figured he hadn't brought any blood-letting weapons. No guns or knives. She wouldn't put it past him to have some other sort of tools. Matches, perhaps a syringe filled with some nondescript drug. She couldn't get too close to him. And at this point, she had to hope she would have enough time between killing the guy and burying him before everyone else got home from work or school.

Hopefully the ground wasn't too frozen.

"You want any tea?" Gertie drifted to the electric kettle atop the counter. Already full, she plugged it in. "Also, the kids made cookies."

"What flavor?"

"Chocolate chip with cinnamon." She pointed to the center of the table, where a ceramic cake stand sat, glass dome on top. A treasure of golden-brown cookies waited for the taking. "River is going to try to make these for the bake sale this spring."

"The boy made them?" He tentatively crunched down on a cookie, and his beard caught some of the crumbles. "Damn, these would've given my nana a run for her money."

Gertie grabbed a couple of mugs from one of the cabinets and some tea bags, lavender and jasmine. She added them to the mugs and once the kettle clicked off, poured a little water into each, then tossed the rest at Earl's face. His hands flew up and he howled in rage. She walked over, picked up the lid to the cake stand, and smashed it across his face. He fell backward against the wall. She dumped the cookies off the stand and lifted the heavy ceramic plate above her head, then rammed it into his skull, bludgeoning him over and over again. He tried to grab her and push her back, but his bloodshot eyes were still simmering from the boiling water. Watermelon seeds of brain matter spattered the wall behind him before he collapsed, dead.

Gertie fished Trevor's finger from Earl's pocket and groaned in frustration when she saw the blood emptying from his skull like a tipped-over punch bowl. She stood there, hovering over the growing mess, her eyes watering with frustration at the amount of work she had to do. His car was parked

148

in her driveway. His body would need to be chopped up and buried in the backyard—and then she'd have to remember to dig up the damn thing in six months and get rid of the bones. In the distant memory of her mother's true crime novels, that was always the thing that damned the serial killers: they never moved the body from where they buried it. But moving this man's body *now* was going to be an issue. She didn't have the strength to drag him into the backyard, not without ruining the carpet by the back door. It had taken her long enough to scrub the stains of Westley from the living room.

She retrieved her trusty meat cleaver, feeling like she was reuniting with an old acquaintance. She set to work, taking it off chunk by chunk, deconstructing the mannequin with extreme care. Sweat gathered underneath her neck and her back creaked in protest after bending over the steaming corpse for so long. She grimaced and cursed, muttering as her hands grew slippery with blood. She nearly nicked herself with the cleaver once or twice.

Lost in her furious reverie, she didn't hear the garage door open.

"Gertrude?"

Her head jerked up, eyes wild, and she saw Bea standing in the doorway to the kitchen. Color drained from her face, her knees buckled as she absorbed the carnage strewn across their kitchen floor like a toddler's art project. Gertie lowered the cleaver and raised her hands. Bea hyperventilated, clapping a hand over her mouth to stifle the shock. After a few moments of panting, she turned to the side and retched. Milky white bile powdered the floor. She must've had the clam chowder from the grocery deli for lunch—something Gertie warned her against several times.

"G-Gertie," Bea gasped. A shaking hand attempted to wipe away the droplets but instead spread it across her face. Viscous snot bubbled in her flaring nostrils. "What in the *fuck* happened?"

Gertie sat, exuding calm, pressing her trembling hands on her knees. "An accident."

"This doesn't look like an accident, honey—oh Jesus, is that my cake stand?"

"I'll buy you a new one."

"That's not the point." Bea belched, but managed to swallow the lump of vomit this time. "How long has he been dead?"

"Maybe like, half an hour?" Gertie arched her brow. "You're home early."

"I got off early," Bea groaned, burying her face in her hands. She shook her head, looked up, then averted her gaze again. "Oh man…"

Gertie's brow furrowed. Here she had expected Bea to run screaming from the house. Maybe reach into the pocket of her cargo pants and whip out her cell phone to dial 911. What was this emotion? When Bea looked up again, she suddenly shrieked in terror, her finger pointing at something. "What the fuck is that?"

*Oh shit.* Trevor's grungy little finger. Gertie plucked it off of Earl's chest, her breathing shallow, suddenly feeling like this was unfamiliar to her.

"It's your son."

"What?" Bea's eyes widened. "He—did he kill—"

"No, Beatrice. I did."

"You...you did what?"

"I killed him."

"Damn." She gnawed on the inside of her cheek, frustrated. "I mean, probably for the best, but..."

Chills overtook Gertie's body. *What?* She stared at Bea in pure confusion, but the woman's expression remained only the slightest bit somber.

"He was a real pain in the ass, you know?" Bea sighed. "But...what made you do it?"

"Because he tried to—he tried to assault June. He..."

"Mmm-hmm. For the best," Bea grumbled with a slow nod, now more comfortable with the idea. "He was taking after his father, and I couldn't stop it. He would've been a real rat bastard. And I wouldn't have wanted anything to happen to June. I adore her." She bit her lip. "But you're not going to kill River, right?"

"Why would I kill River?" Gertie asked. River was so sweet, so sensitive. He reminded her too much of Jack. There was no way she would ever harm a hair on that boy's head. "He's a good kid."

"Ahh, see, I knew. I knew you had your reasons."

Gertie tilted her head to the side like a dog that had heard the treat box shaking. Bea was far too relaxed for this. Almost like—

"I know, Gert. I know about Westley."

"You…"

Bea held up her hands, defensive. "Not the entire time. Just—I noticed the robe I bought for you went missing, and when Trevor was going through that destructive phase, I got the security camera app installed on my phone, so I got access to our cloud. It let me filter for videos that had people in them, and—"

"You saw him on the security cam footage."

"And I figured you might've had a hand in whacking my parents." She gestured to Earl's dead body. "I guess he was the one who helped you pull it off?"

Gertie bit her lip.

Bea nodded, then sighed. "Westley and Trevor, I can wrap my head around," Bea said, her voice hoarse. "But my parents…they were horrible people, but you knew I was relying on them. Did you just do it to get me to move in with you?"

Gertie squeezed her eyes shut. Air rippled through her chest like a skipping stone that had hit water. She licked her lips, parched. "Bea," Gertie whispered, "I have to come clean about something." She rubbed her hands against her thighs, averting her gaze. "I only started dating you because I wanted to get revenge."

"Revenge?" She thought for a moment, confusion ebbing away after a few seconds. "For what happened when we were kids?"

"At first it felt like that. Then it felt like I was getting revenge on life." Frustrated, she closed her eyes. "I lost the plot somewhere along the way."

"But I apologized for what happened, didn't I?"

"You did *not.* You apologized that day in the parking lot, but when we went to Jack and the Bean, you kept going on and on about why you did it. You never said that you were sorry."

"No," Bea whispered. "*No.*"

Rivers of tears streamed from those silver eyes, and the lightning of her pain split her voice in two. In her anguish, Gertie could see it. Bea's white flag. She had gotten revenge, something she had set out to do, something she had convinced herself would bring her so much joy—

—but instead she felt the same as the corpses she had deprecated. Torn apart, bruised, gutted from the inside out. Nothing could hurt more than watching the woman she loved cry from the agony of heartbreak. Pain, she had discovered, was so limiting when it wasn't paired with love.

Her eyes watered as she watched Bea wallow in misery, and she crawled to her, bloody snail trails smearing across the floor. She cupped Bea's face in her hands, gazing deep into those blistered eyes, stroking the stiff bristles of her hair.

Bea hiccuped. "So…you never felt anything for me? It was…all a lie?"

"No," Gertie whispered. "It changed. You changed me. After your parents died, I—you said something to me in the morning that…that made me realize that I *could* love. Maybe I don't do it right. Maybe my love isn't as good as other people's. But that morning, I fell in love with you, Beatrice."

"But do you still resent me for what happened?"

"I…" Gertie was desperate to tell her no. She wanted to bury that fury along with the rest of Earl's corpse and Trevor's festering finger, but her trauma hadn't evaporated. Sometimes when Bea was angry or frustrated, it snapped her right back to that bathroom stall. Life and other people had scarred them, yes, but they had done the same to each other. That was a part of their history that no amount of lovemaking, no whispers in the dead of night, no kiss could wake them from. This was not their fairytale.

This was their nightmare.

"I'm sorry," Gertie buried her face against Bea's shoulder, sobbing. "I don't want to be like this."

"So you're angry? You love me, but you're still angry?"

"Yes."

A solid breath escaped. "Okay."

"Okay?"

"We just need to figure this out." Bea held her at arm's length, wiping away some of her tears. The heartache was gone, replaced with a renewed sense of determination. "We love each other, but you're angry. So how do we make this work?"

Gertie looked over at the mutilated corpse.

Bea waved a dismissive hand. "Don't worry about that right now. Let's talk this out."

"I've done *horrible* things to you, to people that you loved. You—you shouldn't *want* to be with me."

Bea stared at her. "You not loving me scared me, Gertie. This doesn't. If you thought it would, well, you've underestimated the life I've lived."

"You don't understand how bad things have gotten. How much control I've lost. If you're trying to trick me into trusting you so that you can call the cops, then—"

"I'm not calling the cops. I'm trying to have a conversation with you."

"Are you only doing this because you and River need a place to live?"

Hurt flashed across Bea's face. "I'm doing this because I love you, Gertrude. Because you are the only person in this world I will ever fucking love."

Gertie blinked, stupefied. Bea's hands held her face,

cradling her in the same reassuring way they always had. Gertie leaned into her touch, tears dripping from her cheeks. The tangy stench of copper wafted through the air, but even that could not upset her.

"I mean it," Bea whispered. "I love you, and that means loving all parts of you. Even the dark ones."

All this time Gertie thought Bea had evolved, but it was at that moment she realized Bea didn't change from when they were kids. She was just as fucked in the head, but she had changed *how* she loved. She went from demanding total obedience to blissful subservience. Bea was loyal to her in a way that her beloved Jack wasn't. The realization felt like blasphemy, but it was true. Jack was pure. Good. Wholesome. Had she begun this reign of terror when he was still alive, he would have left her. He was her conscience, so with him out of the way, there was nothing to ground her to righteousness.

In contrast, Bea pledged her allegiance with blind faith, and unlike with Jack, Gertie wasn't afraid to ask Bea why she loved her. Bea told her the reasons every single day. She had already experienced the joys of life with this woman ruling by her side, but now she understood that her possibilities could soar beyond what she'd ever dreamed. The school board was only the beginning. She could go for the state legislature, if she wanted to. Hell, maybe she could run for governor.

Maybe this is what true love looked like the second time around.

But at this point, Gertie was unconvinced she was the right person for Bea. Dragging her love into the depths of the hell that she created didn't seem fair. Bea wasn't at the helm of this ship, she was just a passenger along for the ride. She wouldn't have much, if any control, over what course their future took.

"You..." Gertie trailed off. "You know if you stay with me, you're going to have to keep this all a secret, right? This is so much to live with, Bea. Are you sure?"

"Why not?" Bea asked with a laugh. "Do you know the number of bad things I've done for people who *said* they've loved me? The difference is, you actually do."

"You wouldn't want to find someone else? Someone who didn't have baggage? Between the murders, and..." She couldn't even say his name.

"I won't compete with Jack. My love is not that selfish." Bea's eyes were warm, yet piercing. "You have been good to me, Gertie. You do all the things for me that other lovers won't do, just to keep me happy. And you are loyal. You're much too precious for me to ever give up. You'd have to kill me, and even then, that would give me ecstasy. I told you a long time ago you could rip me open from the inside out and I'd love every second of it."

Gertie slumped against the wall, unsure of what to say, so she said nothing.

Bea glanced between them and the corpse. "Do I have

to prove my love to you?"

"How would you prove it?"

"You tell me."

"I don't…" Gertie deflated. "I don't know."

"What would be your innermost desire? The thing that you want most from me."

"Well, your love. But I have that."

"Think about what inspired you to do revenge."

"Hatred."

"Hatred," Bea repeated. "I can work with that." A knowing smirk spread across her lips. "I can work with that, for sure."

"What?"

Bea stood up and entered the kitchen. She reached into an upper cabinet to retrieve a plate. She walked into the bathroom, shut the door, and a few minutes later, re-emerged with a used tampon lying on top of it. The wad of cotton was massive—a super absorbent kind—and was so dark with blood it was almost black. It was a borderline toxic-shock syndrome inducing amount of blood. How Bea was still standing and not going into sepsis amazed Gertie.

Bea locked eyes with her. "Say the word and I'll do it."

But she didn't wait. Gertie shrieked when the woman picked up the tampon by its brown withering string, akin in texture to a drowned rat's tail. She dangled the damp, glistening wad of cotton above her head like it was a clump of grapes on a vine. Inch by inch she lowered it closer to her lips, but Gertie said nothing, just continued to stare in horror.

Bea slurped the object into her mouth and crunched down on the tissue. It moved in her jaw like something with the texture of an aged jerky, gritty and grimy, but slippery when soaked with saliva. Bea had to chew on it for quite a bit in order to break it down into smaller pieces. Juices of coppery blood and something almost unbearably salty filled Bea's mouth. To Gertie's surprise, Bea didn't once gag. She swallowed, and when she did, she beamed at Gertie with pride.

"Satisfied?"

"No!" Gertie cried out in disgust, then shrieked with laughter.

Tears sprung to her eyes and she fell against Bea, who wrapped her arms around her in a loving embrace. She pressed her filthy lips into Gertie's mass of tangled black curls.

"I never ate anything! I spat it out."

"Okay, well, I did the next best thing. Now if you want me to find *more*—"

"Please, God, never do that again," Gertie giggled.

Something inside her felt bubbly—a shaken soda on the verge of bursting. She looked up at Bea, grabbed her chin, and kissed her. Slow and deep. She could taste the blood on her tongue, and for a moment, she wondered if she had ever tasted anything more delicious. Desire stirred low in the pit of her stomach and she tugged on the belt of Bea's jeans.

"You want to take these off so I can return the favor?"

Bea's eyebrows rose, but her smile remained sultry. "What is this, a blood pact?"

"Let's make it one."

# Epilogue

At the sound of her name being called, Gertie stepped up to the podium. She blinked back the onslaught of tears threatening to escape and peered into the crowd of smiling faces and flashing cameras. Here there were only a few hundred people, but one day, she imagined thousands. She greeted them, and they responded with raucous applause before allowing her to speak. Her speech was simple. She had written it in the fifteen-minute car ride over to city hall, but it was all that was needed for them to recapture their love for her. Soon their cheers overpowered her voice.

Laughing, she glanced over her shoulder to look at those who mattered most. June and River, clapping their hands, and Bea, whose smile said it all. Diabolical violence and torture had led them to this moment, but in its chaos, a tender love sprung anew, like a flower in the crevice of a sidewalk. Basking in the glow of everyone's praise, Gertie knew her heart had been healed, and she relished this for a few reasons.

One, because Jack would've been so proud of her for finding new love.

Two, because she had gained a new purpose.

Third? When you had a partner in crime, you were even scarier to fuck with.

## The End

# Acknowledgments

First off, a warm thank you to my beta readers, Billie and Bri, for all of their advice. Bri, you have long been one of my biggest supporters and I am so grateful for your friendship, and your continual readiness to say, "Hell yeah!" to reading whatever messed-up manuscript I've finished.

To Rue, thank you for smiling through every single disturbed story description I've given you these past couple of years, and for supporting me even when it makes you squeamish. To Rachel, thank you for being my cheerleader and encouraging me to keep my head held high when I felt like giving up. To Angela, thank you for your support, feedback, and assistance on research; I always love talking about writing with you (and it helps that you really dig gore.)

A sincere thank you to various individuals in the horror community and writing friends who have been so supportive of me, including but not limited to I.S. Belle and Caitlin Marceau for their wonderful blurbs. Thank you to David-Jack and Lee with Slashic Horror Press for all their support from the get-go and for being so excited about this story, and all your wonderful suggestions on how to make it even better. Also, a big thank you to Ruth Anna Evans for her work on the gorgeous cover.

Finally, a sincere thank you to you, the reader, for your support, and taking a chance on this disturbed, violent, tender little novella.

# About the Author

Minnesota native Chloe Spencer is an award-winning writer, indie gamedev, and filmmaker. She is the author of *Monstersona* and *Duality*. Her work has also been seen in the *Chlorophobia* anthology with Ghost Orchid Press and the *Nightmare Fuel* anthology with Cloaked Press.

In her spare time she enjoys playing video games, trying her best at Pilates, and cuddling with her cats. She holds a BA in Journalism from the University of Oregon and an MFA in Film and Television from SCAD Atlanta.

You can find more about her on www.chloespenceronline.com.